Mountains of Love

Mountains of Love

A STORY OF MEMORIES, PAST LOVES AND NEW ADVENTURES

BRITT HOLLAND

Mountains of Love First published by Arabian Wolf Publications 2021

Arabian Wolf Productions
House of Social Enterprise BV
Geleenstraat 16,2
1078 LE Amsterdam
The Netherlands

First edition

ISBN: 978-1-8383802-1-2

www.brittholland.com

Literary Agent: Susan Mears

Contents

To Susi
For your immediate wholehearted belief in me.
And for the incredible, colourful, and
transformational journey we are on.

From one Soul Sister to another, xxx

Introduction

Vivika, the high flying, fun loving hospitality professional from *Between the Sheets,* attends *The Grand Reunion* in the Swiss Alps. Here she had lived, loved, and learnt with her fellow students, three decades earlier. Vivika wonders whether Bash, her old flame, will attend.

More than memories are rekindled on the Mountain of Love.

Vivika's adventures take a turn for the worse when she is connected with an illegal network.

Will she continue to believe in Bash, or is it time for her to smell the coffee?

As circumstances unfold, Vivika encounters pain and gain, until she begins to write her own future.

Acknowledgements

Thank you Uli, for your unwavering support. From Africa to Europe and back again. From Glam Camp to Eco Hotels, from the mountain where we lived, to the current day. Your input, love, care, suggestions, and inclusions are woven through the fabric of *Mountain of Love*.

Thank you Mummy, Corinne, Imke, Mireille, Anette, Alevtina, Yulia, Jenna, Claire, Ann, Elvira, Alicia, Roweida, Farida, Rosalind, Natalie, Leila, Marjolijn, Jetty, Sue, Nicole, Sandra, Nancy, Sallie, and my other friends and confidantes, who contributed, read, and supported the creation of *Mountains of Love* by giving input, or simply by being part of my life.

Huge thanks to Khaled, Peter and Louca for being heroes.

Thank you too, all my fellow *Mountain Mates* for your inspiration, and for allowing the past to become the present and give way to the future.

Nothing ever happens without the love of my family and My Rock DM.

Thank you for being there, always.

Mountain Magic

The mountains always appeared closer when rain was forecast. They somehow became more solid and dramatic than on sunnier, cloudless days. As if a threat was materialising in an otherwise beautiful landscape. Even though the sunset coloured the rockface pink, a downpour was looming.

You could smell the rain.

It was imminent.

I usually enjoyed going out in the pouring rain. I found it refreshing and invigorating. The cleansing of nature, the touch of the falling raindrops on your skin, the rosy cheeks resulting from being in an oxygen infused outdoor environment all appealed to me. It connected you to your environment. Rather than being a visitor to life, you were immersed and an intrinsic part of it.

On this day, when the rains broke, we were told to stay inside. It was April 26, 1986, a mere month before graduation, the day of the *Chernobyl Disaster*.

The nuclear reactor in the former USSR had blown, and the

radioactivity was penetrating the atmosphere, causing fear and devastation to the immediate area and the rest of the world. The poisonous clouds of destruction travelled west to Europe, passing over the Swiss Alps in the canton of Valais.

Here we lived on top of the Magnificent Mountain, all 239 of us, from 42 different countries worldwide, in our own mini-world, in a former farming community. Sick people suffering from tuberculosis and lung diseases used to convalesce in this place. Large sanatoria with impressively grand balconies the size of squash courts, able to accommodate the patients' beds, offered magnificent views of the resplendent *Dents du Midi*. These seven vertiginous summits of the iconic mountain range changed with the weather.

On some days, the tops of *Les Dents* were hidden from view. Like veiled beauties shrouded in mystery, the seven sisters occasionally offered a glimpse of their beautiful faces as the mist curtain lifted, only to be covered up again from prying eyes as the next robust cloud took charge and blocked out their presence.

The splendour and the glory of *Les Dents* became symbolic for the time of our lives when we lived, learnt, and loved on The Mountain, perched on top of the world in our little corner of French-speaking Switzerland, overlooking the Rhône Valley.

When my neighbour popped her head around the frosted glass screen separating our dorm balconies, I was getting some air.

"Bussi, what are you doing outside? We were told to stay in our rooms because of what happened in Ukraine."

"I am out of the rain, sheltered and not getting wet," I replied.

"Not good enough. Go back inside and let me bring the bottle of white from *Aigle Les Murailles*, the vineyard we always pass by when we drive up the mountain. I picked up a bottle from the supermarket. Let's see if it is any good."

"Great idea but bring the glass from your bathroom. I only have one. Mine is full of toothpaste, so it may be a minty white wine. I ran out of washing up liquid in a failed attempt to get that red wine stain out of my ski suit. I should have chucked a bottle of white at it when it happened, but that seemed like a waste of wine."

"Pass your glass to me," Maddie said. "I have washing powder I use to do my undies. Give me a few minutes as they are soaking in the sink. I will rinse my underwear and then wash both our glasses and pop over with the vino."

I went to get the glass and passed it to Maddie.

"Here you go, my darling neighbour. Promise not to dunk it into your washing. I love you, but I'm not keen on the idea of my glass being swirled around with your smalls. Who knows who else has been there?"

"Buss, what an outrageous insinuation. I am more well behaved than some of our fellow friends here on this mountaintop, I can tell you," she laughed.

"See you in a minute. No need to knock, just come on in."

"Will do, Viv. Close the balcony door, though, *chica*, because I am sure it was not just the rain, but also the air that carries the lurgy. And for today at least, we should follow instructions." Then she added, "Not that we follow the rules normally. See you in a few."

With that, Maddie disappeared out of sight. I went inside to straighten out the duvet on my single bed and light a few candles which I kept stashed in my bottom drawer. The Dutch tradition of lighting candles, whatever the occasion may be, was deeply embedded in me.

I am a blend of cultures. My mum is British, and my father was born in the Netherlands, where I spent most of my growing years. The Dutch habit is to light candles, not just on wintery nights or when guests call round. It appeals to me. Spreading light and creating a positive atmosphere is so simple. Even if you are by yourself, the vibe and energy change with a bit of candlelight.

All the rooms in The Annex were identical in layout. A single bed, a small bathroom with a shower, a desk, two wooden chairs, and a compact wardrobe. Once a week, we stripped our beds and bundled our dirty linen into a ball for the Yugoslavian lady to collect. We left the mattress and pillow covers outside our doors on a Saturday morning to exchange them for fresh ones. I was never sure why the housekeeping manager wanted us to deliver our sheets on Saturday morning, of all mornings. After we had all been out on Friday night, you might well be forgiven for not remembering. If you missed your Saturday *pick up slot*, you were stuffed. You had to wait for the following week.

Some of the diehard party students never made the Saturday pick up and ended up in dubious covers that they slept in during the entire term, and they were not always sleeping alone. During half term, hygiene standards were reset. This was achieved by thoroughly purging, disinfecting, and blitzing all rooms. Many of the accommodations turned into veritable pigsties during term. Crisp packets, condoms - mostly used, empty wine bottles and discarded cotton pads with makeup on them littered the rooms. Sometimes a hidden and forgotten joint was found; always a delight for the cleaners.

A knock, or rather, a kick on the door.

"Come in," I said.

Maddie entered, holding the wine bottle, a corkscrew and both our toothbrush glasses.

"I thought I told you no need to knock or kick I should say."

"I know, but I am still half German, Bussi, and it is embedded in me. I may be a bit Italian in other ways, but my Germanic side surfaces when things must be done a certain way. Then my Italian half challenges my German side. I end up being a bit mixed up," she laughed. "And as for my kicking instead of knocking, I have my hands full, so that's why."

"Come in, my dear. I know the feeling of being a blend of two cultures. My British mother thinks it is OK to use only her fork when having supper at home. My Dutch dad says that fork and knife are required, except when you are eating chunky fries or *patat,* then it is fine to use fingers, which my mother thinks is unacceptable. My mum puts the salt on the side of the plate, and my father sprinkles it over his food. In Dutch culture, you put both your hands on the table after eating, while in England, you put them in your lap under the table. No wonder we are mixed up. It is also a great thing to use cultural differences to justify your manners, depending on what suits you best at the time. Lucky we are in Switzerland, which has a reputation for being neutral. Besides, with forty-two nationalities, we can lock into whatever cultural rule we like. Mix it up, I say! Now let's try that white you brought round."

Maddie is from Berlin. She enlightened me by telling me that a *Berliner* is a doughnut with jam on the inside. By using *ein* before the word Berliner, JF Kennedy mistakenly called himself a jelly doughnut during his famous speech delivered on June 26, 1963, against the geopolitical backdrop of the Berlin Wall, when he said, *'Ich bin ein Berliner.'*

After the Kennedy Story, Maddie always returned from her holidays with a large box of *Berliners*, which we would chomp through over tea as we caught up with each other's news. It became a ritual. We called each other a '*Berliner*' or 'doughnut' if either of us was behaving like a numpty or if we did something seriously unintelligent or ridiculous.

In terms of education, having our very own 'United Nations' on top of one mountain was as important as our hospitality management. Our day to day life included learning about and respecting intercultural habits. Sometimes when we returned from a party just before dawn, Ibrahim and Omar could be found on their individual prayer mats facing the direction of Mecca. No matter what time they made it back from the disco, they were committed to praying Fajr. I was in awe of that level of discipline. No matter how hard you played, as a Muslim, you prayed. We were all different due to our backgrounds, beliefs, and upbringing, though, in the scheme of things, we were incredibly similar. As are all humans.

That was when I learnt about Islam as well as other faiths.

One day, Lisa refused Maddie and my entry into her room. We were both munching on chocolate-covered biscuits as we arrived at Lisa's place to complete a team task, brandishing the rest of the roll to share with the team.

"No cookies allowed," Lisa said. "So sorry, darlings, I can't let you in." She added, "No crumbs."

Maddie and I were confused.

"It's Passover, my dears. I tried my best to clean my room for the occasion. Trying to make my Jewish mother proud, hundreds of miles away from this mountaintop. She will never believe me when I tell her, so I am not entirely clear as to who I am doing this for." She laughed. "Though the big guy in the sky will notice, I guess."

"We know you never let a carb pass your lips, so we will make ourselves and our cookies scarce. Sorry, we didn't know. Let's change our plan and meet at mine," I said.

That's how I learnt about Passover as well as other traditions and occasions.

Albert, a fellow student, used to have his own habit. While we were having our morning coffee in the bar, he always ordered a whiskey. This was not culturally motivated but rather an unfortunate addiction that we were all worried about. Albert was a lovely chap, but it seemed that whatever his pain was, he could only dull it down with his daily fix of an early morning potent potion. Little did we know that we would lose Albert prematurely, as well as some of our other most colourful and kind friends, for a variety of sad reasons.

That was life as we learnt it the hard, and only, way.

We had regular events that we called *National Nights*. During those evenings, the students from a particular country or region clubbed together to present their food, dances, delicacies, culture, and traditions. Our fellow students from Asia performed magnificent dances during Asian Night. Some of the students sat in crouched positions and moved massive bamboo poles, between which the other Asian students danced in a most impressive ritualistic performance. The key performer,

Anis, sparkled and shone.

Anis was my idea of a true creative. He was an old soul with a young artistic heart. He seduced boundaries to create beauty; he was not a hostage to strict tradition. Although his outfit was predominantly of an Asian design, his silk clothes matched with the many deep gold coloured bangles and sequinned turban, evoking an Arabian Nights' kind of vibe. Anis moved elegantly between the bamboo poles, graciously yet deliberately controlling his limbs, synchronising his hand and finger movements simultaneously. He could be described as quiet, timid even, until he was dancing and performing to his heart's content, eyes shining as he moved.

After Anis's mesmerising performance, an impressive Chinese dragon snaked through the canteen. The Chinese Embassy sponsored the evening and included this beast of bright greens and reds. The Dragon Dance was typically performed by experienced dancers who manipulated the figure. They would have poles at regular intervals along the length of the dragon. As Dr Google informed me, the dragon dance is believed to bring good luck. The dragon is supposed to symbolise great power, dignity, and wisdom. The dancers are meant to simulate imagined movements of the river spirit in an undulating manner.

Ayla's deliberate movement led the beast's front, but the tail-end had Kim continuously trying to get back into the meandering creature made of cloth. Kim was the last of five students to manipulate the snake movements of the dragon; he was also the largest and least nimble.

We all thought it was hilarious, of course, and encouraged him, "Come on, Kim, catch up with the ass of the Dragon!"

In the end, he gave up, and the tail end of the dragon was

dragged limply along the floor. Kim had given up on his responsibility of bringing luck through dance and went to indulge in some Dim Sum instead, along with a bottle of *Tiger Beer* from Singapore. Also sponsored. I must say the Asian Embassies came up trumps. The event was a total hit.

The canteen area was usually drab, though, for the event, it was decorated with lanterns of every colour and size and was absolutely transformed. The Asian Night was topped off with a magnificent firework display, thanks again to the Chinese connections. The burst of colours in the dark sky reflected in our eyes as we stood side by side on the oversized balconies, looking up at the exploding colours. It was on this magical mountain in the Swiss Alps that Forever Friendships were forged.

It was strange how I ended up at Hotel school. I had no interest whatsoever in working in hotels. Operations, logistics, standard operating procedures, rules, and regulations were the very things that stifled me. Just the thought of them made my throat go dry.

So boring!

My personal interest was *languages*. I enjoyed French and Spanish, more so than German, which I felt was rigid and controlled. Spanish had flair and appeal. Spanish men sounded as if they had drunk whiskey and been smoking heavy tobacco since early adolescence. Their voices reverberated deeply as they spoke, their words projected with great speed and passion. Then, they'd stop to inhale their cigarettes. And give you *that look*. The one that left you speechless. The Spanish know how to communicate beyond language. Passionately and eloquently. I was mesmerised by their ability to make you listen and convey what was never said. The way people interpret words or never use them yet still communicate with dramatic effect has always fascinated me.

The ability to communicate with other people allows for a whole new opportunity to explore life. During my time at Hotel Management School, I was also introduced to Arabic. Maybe that new interest had more to do with the Iraqi-Syrian guy who'd caught my fancy. He did teach me a thing or two along the way, though perhaps not precisely related to the spoken language.

Coco, who was one of my friends growing up, was petite. She was 150.5 cm tall, as she often liked to remind us. That half a centimetre made all the difference in her book. Her hallmarks were determination, grit, drive, and perseverance. Coco wanted to study hotel management and went on a mission to find her school. She researched available institutions, shortlisted them, made appointments and then set off to drive herself from Holland to Switzerland to meet the Directors and student bodies of all the shortlisted establishments. She concluded her choice and signed up. When Coco told me about her selected school and showed me the brochure, I knew. The energy oozed from the pages of the booklet. This was it. Not a university in the Netherlands which spelt 'same, same,' to me, but an adventure, a new horizon, a welcome proposition. I spoke to my mother and showed her the pamphlet and the curriculum. As well as the prices, which were as steep as the surrounding mountains.

My mum looked me in the eye and said, "Vivi, darling, I think this is it. There is no way we could agree to this in normal circumstances, but I am working at a well-paid job that will continue for some time. So, if daddy agrees and if you are truly committed to this, we can perhaps find a way to make this work."

I was over the moon. As if all the pieces of the puzzle had fallen into place. I knew I was privileged to start my further education and change my surroundings and gain new experiences.

My parents drove me to Switzerland. It was a nine-hour journey from where we lived in Amsterdam. My parents naturally sat in the front, and I sat in the back, snoozing, chatting, and looking around. On the motorway in Germany, a massive truck was driving next to us. From his vantage point up high, the lorry driver looked down into our car. He saw me sitting on the back seat with my feet up on the chair in front of me, with my dress hitched up for comfort. Naturally, I was not expecting anyone to observe me. So, when I clocked him leering down at me, I immediately gave him one of my '*go and play in the traffic, old pervert*' glances and at the same time gave him my pronounced middle finger. I was pleased that my father picked up speed though he was not aware of what was going on in the backseat of the car and the lorry driver beside us. The sad-head behind the wheel seemed to be warming up to this *Motorway Intermezzo*. We managed to move ahead, and I thought the annoyance had passed until the bloke caught up with us again and tried to stay alongside our car. My father and mother noticed the continued presence of the truck and started commenting. In the end, I had to come clean that I had given him the bird. My dad eventually managed to shake him off when he veered off the motorway at the last minute to get petrol, and the truck continued onwards.

I think we didn't really need any petrol; it was a break to reset and for my parents to reinforce that there were going to be '*All-Sorts*' out there and keep my cool and pick my fights. That I should think before I act. *Spontaneous responses* have always been my problem.

I am a bit impromptu at times, shall we say.

We snaked our way up the mountain towards where the school was located. As we arrived, many people were coming and going. I saw one girl, smoking, with her arm around a guy, both holding tennis racquets and laughing. That was Hélène.

Many years later, I would become her neighbour in Amsterdam.

Expensive looking cars dropped students off. In retrospect, I think I was one of the few whose family didn't own an island or run a coffee emporium, oil field or a Fortune500 company. I noted there seemed to be a level of wealth, but it didn't threaten or overwhelm me. We were brought up in comfort and with all we needed. We had friends and family who lived at a higher standard, materialistically speaking, and those who had far less. It was never a thing in our family. All people are equal in spirit, soul, creed, background, and heritage. I was not impressed nor phased by wealth nor a lack of it. I was simply grateful for having been allowed to become whoever I was going to be eventually and blossom into being me.

My parents looked around the school. They met some of the other parents and were introduced to some of the teachers. We went for a *good-luck* dinner. Coco joined us. Afterwards, we said our goodbyes which were a bit hard, but Coco took me to settle into the room we would be sharing. My parents set off down the mountain to their hotel. They planned to drive back to Holland in the early morning.

Brand New World

I woke up early and stepped out onto the balcony.

The mountains across the valley merged with the apple green grass. It was the colour of well-ripened Granny Smiths and looked artificial like the grass in a trainset. I imagined this vibrant tone of green only to be possible if it was manmade. That, I realised soon enough, was flawed thinking. As I stepped out into the world, I became increasingly aware of the grandeur of Mother Nature. She combines purples and oranges and puts together green and blue hues and other unlikely pairings that clash in an artificial world. In the majestic natural setting, however, anything Mother Nature puts together makes sense, gives energy and is always in balance. Why do we not learn that from a young age, I wonder?

Appreciating the obvious early on was a joy that should not be postponed or realised too late in life.

Coco and I shared a room, which was fine. Even though I was keen on my own space, we made it work. One day she sat me down and offered me a cup of coffee brewed in her bright red coffee percolator, the one that made the sound of a clapped out car with a hole in the exhaust.

She lit up a cigarette, inhaling it as if she'd been smoking from early childhood onwards, and said, "Viv, we have been friends for a long time. I love sharing a room with you, but I think I will need some privacy from time to time. I like a guy, but naturally, it will be a bit uncomfortable to bring him here if you don't know we are in the room. Being caught in the act would not be good for you. Nor for me."

With that, she pulled out a scarlet ribbon and held it up next to her head, then she let it fall to touch the floor.

"If either of us needs privacy, for whatever reason, then we will create a *Red Ribbon Moment* by attaching it to the door. That way, we know not to go in until the ribbon has been removed."

From that moment onwards, to 'Red Ribbon', someone was a code understood by all in our building.

Boys were not allowed in the Annex. Naturally, we would sneak them in from time to time if there was a dorm party. We would either wait until Mr Jankovic, the janitor, was out or overcome that barrier by tying a sheet to the desk inside the room on the first floor. From the lowest balcony, the boys could climb up into the Annex.

During the day, we did not expect nor want boys to be around. That was our time; A girl-only zone. We had showers in our room, but you had to go down the corridor if you wanted a bath. Typically, we left the door open as we had our soak. As we chatted, it was not uncommon to share a glass of wine while one person was in the tub and the other sat on the edge.

One day Maddie was coming out of the bathroom carrying a small towel with her. As she walked along the corridor, naked, she was faced with a random guy coming up the stairs and making his way towards her. The oversized flannel Maddie was holding was only big enough to cover either her boobs or her bits below. Not knowing what to choose, she opted to cover her face as she walked in perfect splendour down the corridor and disappeared into her room. Class, confidence, and creative ingenuity. Those were the qualities I associated with Maddie, my dearest neighbour in crime.

On my twenty-first birthday, Maddie invited me to the Top Pub for a drink. After an hour or two, she said we should go back to the Annex as she had to study. I was OK with that, and we strolled down the road. When we got back to the Annex, we passed Maddie's door, covered with a big white paper banner saying, '*Come in, Vivikins! Happy 21st!!!*'

I looked at Maddie, confused.

"Come on in for a birthday drink and then go to your room," Maddie smiled. "I know it may not be much, but I thought a bit of my handicraft would serve as my version of a birthday card. Punch your way in, Viv and open the door to your new year."

Laughing, I put my fist through the paper and opened the door, immediately realising what was happening.

"SURPRISE!!!" my friends cheered as they sprayed Champagne over me when I entered, and they leapt forward for hugs, filling my hands and arms with cards, flowers, and bubbly.

It was such a lovely and generous initiative. The boys

clambered over the balcony, except for Karl, who we sneaked in via the fire escape. Karl seemed happy enough though he was totally disoriented. We had been skiing that afternoon. Theo, my Dutch friend from Costa Rica, who was like a brother to me and Alex and Karl, went off-piste. Karl had experienced an unfortunate accident. He overlooked a massive snow mogul and had skied straight into it. As a result, he'd passed out.

When he came round, he kept saying, "I rang my bell, I rang my bell. Ding-dong!"

Karl's girlfriend Majida was Swedish. Her mother, a platinum blond vision of elegance, worked for Scandinavian Airlines as cabin crew when she found out she was pregnant with Majida. As her mother was in Oman at the time, she chose an Arabic name for her baby girl, and that's how Majida got landed with her first name.

Karl did not appear concussed though he was confused. He went from skiing at a reasonable speed to a total standstill in one split second. When Majida tried to comfort Karl, he had no idea who she was.

Bemused, she told him, "But Karl, I am your long-term girlfriend; it's me, Majida!"

"I have no idea who you are," Karl said, "but you are certainly gorgeous. All I can say is that you could be telling me anything, but what I can tell you is *ding-dong, let's do this!*"

Majida was utterly distraught and went off in tears, leaving Theo and Alex in fits of laughter.

Maddie and I were aligned in terms of energy and were always concocting mini-expeditions and possible ventures. One December, not too long before we were going to split up for

Christmas, the snow was falling, thick and fast. We decided we should get a Christmas tree and rig it up in the Annex for Mr Jancovic and fellow students. They would not be able to make it back home over the winter break. When Mr Jankovic wasn't looking, we borrowed the saw and a torch from his workshop and set off in our snow boots, hats, gloves, and warm clothes into the woods, just beyond the Top Pub. We selected a perfectly funky looking Christmas tree, and Maddie, wearing her boots and in her woolly tights and skirt, proceeded to saw it down. It was illegal, of course. At the time, we were not environmentally aware, just pleased as punch that we had found a perfect specimen. We lugged it into the back of Lisa's Jeep, which had winter tyres on it. Without those tyres, we would have got stuck for sure. We set off back to the Annex, where we unloaded the fresh little pine tree and rigged it up in the hallway. We clubbed together in my room, and we cut up our old exams to make paper chains, adding a bit of glue and glitter from our supplies. Later that night, the boys dropped by with their contribution: a five-meter string with beer bottle tops, pop tops, and corks dangling from it.

The bottle tops had been pierced by driving a nail through them. The boys told us that they'd tried shooting through the metal with Bash's air rifle. I was never clear as to the reason why Bash had to keep one of those, but what did we care at that time. I had some fairy lights in my bottom drawer alongside my candles. I referred to it as my '*Let There Be Light Drawer*'. I had used the string of miniature lights previously to decorate my balcony. Still, they weren't waterproof, so I had taken them down. Using them for their actual purpose seemed like an inspired idea.

We held our various Christmas drinks around the tree and rigged up an impromptu sound system to play Christmas rock tunes. We secured a large bunch of Mistletoe tied with Coco's red ribbon above the entrance, so it could not be missed. When the boys arrived, we allowed them to pass under the Mistletoe rather than scaling the balcony. That way, we could better vet which one may be worthy of a little festive Christmas snog on arrival.

"You can borrow my red ribbon," Coco offered, "but if I score under the Mistletoe and land my beau in the sack for a Merry Christmas romp, I will want my red ribbon back to play with my boy-gift undisturbed for an hour or two."

"No worries, Co. Slide away to your heart's content," I laughed. "But why don't you join us for a whole other type of action that involves slippery conditions too. We are off to the canteen to steal some trays. The snow is good. Are you in?"

Coco didn't hesitate.

"Who else is going? It has been a long time. I would love a go at that again. The thrill of it. So simple yet so utterly awesome. Oh my God, excellent idea!"

"Let's meet outside the bar in fifteen minutes. We will split up and divide tasks. Maddie and I will nab the trays, Lisa will go and grab the black sacks, and you and Majida keep the coast clear so we can do what is needed. If anyone comes, distract them, or cause a diversion. You are the queen of distractions, so that's your job. Once we have the equipment, we will regroup outside, up the steps, where Maddie's car is parked. Not that you can see it now because it's covered in snow, but you know where I mean."

We gathered a quarter of an hour later, wearing our snow

boots, gloves, and hats. Coco was sporting a Balaklava. Clearly, she was into the mission at hand and taking matters seriously. We were about to move when Neil, the computer teacher, walked by. We had nicknamed him GDF, meaning *'Gorgeous Dimple Features'*. He always had a healthy ski suntan and dressed in slacks that hugged his muscled ski-bum-behind. We were all convinced that GDF was not there so much to teach as to be paid to ski. He was good at his job. Probably as he related to us and made computer science a class to look forward to. We wouldn't mind poring over more than data with this handsome guy, who was only just over twenty-five himself. However, he was still firmly in the teacher camp and, as a result, both out of bounds and doubly attractive to us. He was good fun and much more relaxed than Mr Neuhaus, a former sergeant-major, who barked at us and made us run in the snow up the steps leading from the top to the bottom in the village.

Neuhaus didn't like the fact that we were not optimally engaged in his class. Only Kim, a descendant from an Asian dynasty, was positively contributing during the lesson. Neuhaus taught us Food and Beverage, as well as Economics. One day the subject was the *'Maslow Pyramid'*. According to the theory, which has since been found lacking, there were five categories of needs: physiological, safety, love, esteem, and self-actual-isation. Neuhaus explained that only when the basic needs of food and shelter had been fulfilled could the other needs emerge and be satisfied. To illustrate the idea, Neuhaus asked the class what a basic was.

"Bread and potatoes," Lisa said. She may have been Dutch, but she categorically never touched any carbs. Ever. Not just during Passover.

"Lice," Kim called out. "We all need lice. That was our basic food in Asia."

We all loved Kim, but it was funny, and we laughed. Rather than saying 'rice', Kim said 'lice'. I am never quite sure why some Asian people swapped the R for L and vice versa.

"Where would that leave Ralph Lauren?" Coco joked.

"Let us meet in the *robby* of the hotel," I quipped.

We were starting to get into it when Neuhaus stood perfectly still in front of the class. It took some of us a bit longer than others to notice that the former sergeant-major had failed to see the funny side. Once, we were all quiet, he spoke with force.

"You are men and women who will lead teams. You will be dealing with different cultures, personalities, and characters. I am quite categorically sure that you have no idea about the basic needs in the Maslow Pyramid. Most of you were born with a silver spoon in your blabbing mouths and have no idea what real work and commitment are. You young hormonal excuses of human beings are concerned about is fulfilling your indulgent attention needs. You appear to have no desire to be upstanding individuals who respect discipline, and you lack resolve. You are wasting my time in my class, being disrespectful and undisciplined. So, you sorry bunch of Future Hospitality Leaders, close your books and stand up, form a line and follow me."

We were all a bit bemused.

What was Neuhaus planning? Where was he taking us?

We followed him down the corridor and broke into a trot as Neuhaus picked up pace in front of us. When we got to the front door, he set off running through the snow, instructing us to follow him. You would not choose to cross Neuhaus.

He was a small, compact, dark bearded man who ruled our class with an iron rod. He could make you shudder in your snow boots. Nobody ever contemplated skiving off to go skiing during his class. No matter that the conditions might be perfect.

"Come on, *Weaklings*," he barked like a bulldog.

From the top of the steps leading up from the school towards the road, he stood looking down on us with disdain as we scaled the stairs. We eventually made it up to where he commanded us from. Most of us were totally out of breath, apart from Dimitri. He was *Mr Fitness Personified* and relished the challenge at hand. He was Russian. Discipline, the need for sports and achievement were embedded in him. Neuhaus did not have the emotional capacity to have favourites. However, I suspect that there was at least a level of relief for Neuhaus. Dimitri at least showed some of the grit the former sergeant-major was looking for.

We stood there like a steaming herd of sheep. We did not have coats on, as Neuhaus had ordered us to go outside. We'd left everything behind, like when you're on a flight in an emergency. You must leave in a hurry and leave your belongings and just follow instructions.

Take high heeled shoes off.

Some of the girls were wearing relatively high heeled shoes. There were rules around the height of your heels, the colour of your nails, as well as other restrictions. We took every opportunity to push our boundaries to be more individual and bolder. Some students tried to be sexier and more attractive in their own mind's eye and that of the appreciative, impressionable boys. Even so, we'd usually be sent back to change, remove, or adjust our outfits to present ourselves within the confined dress code parameters.

Once we'd caught our breath and began to cool down from the climb, we got ready to make our way down the road, back to school.

"Where do you think you are going?" Neuhaus bellowed as we set off down the road. "Were you given permission to leave?"

We were taken aback. We turned to look at Neuhaus, and he gestured to us to come back and then, in a fluid movement, he pointed up the mountain, where the next level of steps loomed in the snow.

"Get on with it!" he shouted. "Get up there and don't dare stop until you reach the top. For those who reach it, return to class, and start your work. And be very sure that if I detect any disrespect or lack of focus, even if from one person only, you will all have more steps to face."

With that, his compact muscled frame bounced up the steps effortlessly in front of us.

"Sadist," I heard Maddie say under her breath.

I was tempted to laugh but didn't dare, so I just kept going, biting my lip, and digging my nails into my hands to stop myself from cracking up.

We felt lucky as we carried out our mission when we happened to run into the lovely Neil outside the canteen, not Neuhaus.

"Hello ladies, up to mischief, are you?" His dimples were even more pronounced as he grinned at us.

As if he'd just read my mind, he said, "Lucky it wasn't a certain sergeant-major you might have run into, ladies. Whatever you are doing, I hope you are enjoying yourselves. You only live once, and you may as well get going with living your life fully. And that includes impromptu initiatives. Will leave you to it."

We beamed at him. We adored Neil, and boy was he to die for.

"Right. Are you mission ready?" I asked my friends.

Lisa, Maddie, Coco and Majida all nodded.

"Affirmative," Coco responded, falling into a salute, with only her green eyes poking excitedly out of the assigned eye sockets in her Balaklava.

She looked like she'd escaped from the Army Seals. Wearing dark colours so as not to be noticed on her mission and ready for potential combat. Though her rationale was flawed. In the current snowscape she would stand out rather than blend in. But Coco was prepared for the mission, committed to conquering, her green eyes blazing.

Majida, by contrast with Coco's outfit, wore a bright pink puffer jacket with mink trim. The top was paired with cream ski culottes with a design of a giraffe on skis, graffiti style. It was a brand that was doing well and was started by her mum, who specialised in upscale Scandinavian Designer Outdoor clothes, especially for skiing and hunting. The hunting was not politically correct, though Majida looked like a divine snow angel in her *Giraffe Graffitis*. I sometimes wondered whether Majida's mum had sent her daughter to school on the mountain just to promote her clothing business.

Majida was beautiful, sporty, and a perfect model to show off her mother's designs.

"OK, see you at the top of the steps in five minutes. Go in, be quick, discreet and remember, no distractions. We need trays and five bin liners. Otherwise, the mission is off," I said.

Seven minutes later, due to a slight delay in opening the fire escape door at the back of the canteen, we regrouped in our agreed spot. The loot was in. One of the trays had a crack in it though it was still usable, and we had five black sacks.

"Great work, ladies. Let's go. Be careful on your descent. The force of gravity will make you ramp-up speed quickly, and we have no brakes apart from our feet. Remember to always find the next possible emergency exit. Contingency plan and think ahead if you go too fast. Steer with your fists and keep your head up and your torso centred."

We each took a tray and slipped it into a plastic bag, gathering any excess plastic and stuffing it under our tummies. We lay down face forward on our DIY *snow sliders.*

At the point where the ascending road meets the descending one, we lined up. In turn, we began edging over the rim as we took turns to slide down the snow-covered road. There weren't many cars on it, though the odd one passed by.

We picked up speed. Steering with our fists and braking with our snow boots, we set off on our thrilling slide down the longest, least winding road in the village. The snow-covered asphalt lay mere centimetres below us as we travelled at speed, laughing our heads off and struggling to keep our balance and direction. The route took a sharp bend at the *téléferique* station. Where the road went up to the lift, you could swing up into the ski-lift area. This allowed you to reduce your velocity to the degree that you could come to a complete stop.

After our adrenaline-filled *joy-ride-on-trays,* we landed intact at the ski-lift. We were not ready to go home just yet. We parked our trays and sacks and whipped out our season ski passes, which we carried with us in case of impromptu missions up the mountain. With a sense of accomplishment, we piled into the arriving lift, the size of a small living room, which would take us up the steep mountain. Twelve minutes later, we arrived, on top of the world with the most incredible view and the best *salade verte* and wine we could wish for. We spent a glorious afternoon in the sunshine, chilling, laughing, and listening to Coco. She told us about her potential new conquest, *Red Ribbon Reinard*, a new ski teacher who was in his first season and had recently arrived on the Mountain of Love.

"I plan to teach him the ropes," Coco announced, even though she had not yet met her unsuspecting victim. But she would. She had her ways. And those green eyes of hers could seduce most men and any '*Moniteur de ski*'.

Blond Boys

Among the people who did not go home for Christmas was my friend Theo. Tall, blond, and good fun, Theo had a particular pose that you would recognise anywhere. He always held his beer clutched to his chest, almost hiding it under his armpit. It was his signature stance. A *cerveza* tucked under and a broad smile on his face, he looked like butter wouldn't melt.

I imagined Theo to be a relatively '*Good Boy*' when I first met him. The type who would not yet have slept with a girl at nineteen and was just the friendly type. We got on very well. I had never fancied him. When I later found out that girls threw themselves at Theo, I was stunned.

We became firm friends while Theo was actively dating a wide variety of girls, not just from our school but from the American College too. I found out that he organised hooker parties in the jungle back home in Costa Rica. He had a girlfriend who was a native Costa Rican. She lived in a tribe in the wilderness. They would go canoeing in a hollowed-out tree trunk and make love behind the wigwam. He told me about jade traders who used to pass through and how they were the ones asking for women in the jungle. Theo was their pimp, it seemed back in Costa Rica.

The Blond Chief of Entertainment.

I took it with a pinch of salt. I never saw Theo as a bad guy. Slightly off centre, sure. But a baddy? No, I didn't think so.

Theo did not hold my attention, but Bash did. He was a blond, blue-eyed, cheeky Arab. His mother was Syrian, and his father was Iraqi. His skin was scarred in an attractive sort of way. I don't know whether it was from acne or something else, but it made him look like a rugged rogue. Raw and male, even though he was only twenty. He loved cars and had two on the mountain. One was a Mustang, the other was the latest Range Rover They were parked in the only garage available at the school. I wondered how Bash had managed to secure those car parking spaces. The Directors of the school parked outside even though the garage was connected to their home. They lived at the end of the old sanatorium building in the Directors' residential wing.

Bash was not the best looking guy in the school.

That title went to Johnny from the Dominican Republic. He moved like a god, smiled like a prince, and would salsa like he was making love. He had looks, rhythm and charm. Girls swooned over him, except for Maddie and me. We liked the more individual types. Bash was one of those. He joked, flirted, and charmed. But he never said much of consequence. We really didn't know much about him. If you asked a direct question, Bash responded with one of his own.

If I suggested an angle and wanted his perspective, he hugged me. He'd say, "Vivikaaaaahhhhh, why all your questions, always, *ya habibti.*"

I loved it when he called me *sweetheart* in Arabic. I never really had a fling with Bash, but there was always an attraction and tension between us. He once pulled me into him in the school disco on a Friday night. I smelled the alcohol on his breath as he nuzzled my neck and said, quite loudly to counteract the music, that he wanted to be with me, but Theo had said he would kill Bash if he touched me. I recall thinking that was odd. As I said, Theo and I were not sexually attracted to one another.

Why, then, did Theo not want me to connect with Bash in that way?

When I asked Theo about it, he kissed my head and said, "*Zusje, Bash is mijn vriend, maar hij is gevaarlijk. Ik kijk uit voor jou.*" Meaning, "Little sister, Bash is my friend, but he is dangerous. I am looking out for you."

I just shrugged it off.

I fancied Bash even though Theo was not smitten with him. I was quite happy not to make a thing of it. Though Theo's words did strike me as odd. Later, I would learn what Theo had meant. The danger was looming, but not until I was to meet Bash again thirty years later.

We had two magical years on The Mountain.

Relations were forged, exams were passed or failed, lessons were learnt, and lives were lived.

I must admit that I had never worked as hard as I did at the Hotel Management Institution of Higher Education. I passed with flying colours, delighting my parents, who had never seen me as focused and committed. I had grown up. I realised I was lucky to have been given this opportunity. This achievement was for me rather than anyone else. However, I was happy that it made my parents proud.

In May 1986, we graduated. The official ceremony took place in the church in the village. The Graduation Ball was held at *Montreux Palace* on the lake, which naturally was cause for a lot of excitement. We got dolled up in our fancy outfits. We made our way in buses, into the Rhône Valley, towards the exquisite hotel. The sun set over Lake Geneva while were drinking our cocktails. As we entered the ballroom, the lights were dimmed as the candles glowed in the darkened space. The ceiling roses and paintings couldn't be clearly seen, though the grandeur of the space was palpable. It was like walking into an elaborate and finely decorated wedding cake.

The sense of celebration and ceremony were all around.

I walked next to Amilcar, who we all thought was a shy Latin American guy, as we went in. He never said much. But still waters run deep.

On entering the ballroom, Amilcar looked at me, smiled his gentle smile and took my hand. I was stunned yet charmed. He never said a word. We walked down in between the large round tables until we reached our places. He squeezed my hand before he let it go. He sat in his place, and I sat in mine, at different tables and according to the table plan.

Amilcar's gentle and unexpected gesture was etched in my mind. I sometimes wondered why it was my hand he held. Perhaps it was because we went into the Grand Ballroom at the same time.

Amilcar was not like the other guys.
Was he gay?
My 21-year-old brain could not work it out.

I knew he was a friend of Theo's, although they could not have been more different. Theo was naughty, and Amilcar was nice. Or so it seemed on the face of it.

When my best friends Annie, Hélène and I travelled to Costa Rica years later, we looked Amilcar up. We swam in the waterfall on his perfect paradise Coffee Estate. He was still quiet, charming, and gentle. And clearly very wealthy. The plantation was enormous, and the art around the house exquisite. Mayan masks, jade, gold, antiquities, and paintings graced *La Hacienda Sueños en el Cielo,* translated as *Dreams in Heaven.* Tastefully decorated with what was referred to as 'Pre-Columbian Art'. Innumerable pieces adorned the *Hacienda.* The beautiful space felt like an illegal museum, bursting at the seams.

Theo joined us at Amilcar's impressive estate.

After a great afternoon with my friends Annie, Hélène, Theo and Amilcar, by the pool, Theo swam over and asked me to join him inside. He climbed nimbly out of the pool. I got out by using the ascending steps. Still dripping, I put my kaftan on over my head and went to join Theo. He put his arm around my shoulder, and we walked together into the massive house. He stopped and stood in the middle of the circular lobby, which boasted a dark and beautiful, tropical hardwood floor. There was no wall between the reception area of Amilcar's house and the coffee plantation and mountains beyond. Theo invited me to take a seat on the comfortable sofa. As he sat next to me, the skies opened.

The rains can start just like that in Costa Rica. Fluffy white clouds can transform into deep, dark, dramatic ones within minutes, dumping their humid overload. After a short downpour, the sky will lift and then turn back to being bright and blue, as if nothing has happened.

The world feels cleaner and more energised after the watershed.

Both the noise and the scent of the rain are aspects I most love about Costa Rica. Mother Nature pours her heart out, and the green vegetation and animals seem to praise her glory.

"*Hermano mio*, what's going on? We left our buddies outside. Is anything wrong?"

"No," Theo replied. "On the contrary. You are my sister, and I want to celebrate that you are in your Costa Rican homeland. It was my deep wish that you would be my sister forever."

I started laughing, "You are pretty solemn, my friend; spill those coffee beans, what's up?"

"Close your eyes and open the palm of your right hand."

I did as Theo asked. I could feel him placing something that felt like a smooth piece of stone, alabaster perhaps, in my palm. I kept my eyes closed and picked up on the pulsating sensation in my hand.

With my eyes still closed, I asked, "Theo, what is this? I can feel incredible energy."

"Vivi, the place where this comes from is not clean. I need you to know that. It is a relic that has been stolen. But by giving it to you, because you have a clean heart and it is intended for a pure soul, it will be cleared from anything bad."

"Oh, my Lord," I whispered. "What is this?"

"Open your eyes and see. Most importantly, know it is given to you with love, and that negates any bad energy. This little man will bring you luck. Open your eyes and see."

I did as Theo instructed me.

There in my hand was the most perfect little Mayan Man looking up at me. Carved from jade, the colour of vibrant emerald, he had a triangular nose etched into the stone. Halfway down the figurine, five lines were carved out on each side that represented his fingers. At the bottom of the mini jade sculpture, there were similar lines that portrayed his toes. The amulet had an energy, a pulse, and an aura that left me speechless.

"He is yours," Theo told me as he kissed me on my forehead. "You deserve always to be watched over. And while I am sure our dear *Dios* above keeps an eye on you, as you are a good person, you need a little help from your friends and extended family."

I was baffled. "This little man is utterly divine, Theo, but where is he from?"

"Don't ask, Vivi. Just know he is yours now. All energies have been purified. Because you are good, and he was given to you with clear and clean intentions."

"Thank you," I said as I gave Theo a big hug. It was nice to know we were such close friends. Nothing else beyond our friendship had ever been important to us, and nothing else ever would be.

"The figurine is made from the purest of jade and is pre-Columbian. Look after him."

I held the little man in my hand, and then, because I had no pockets, I popped him into the bra of my swimsuit where he was wedged snugly against my skin.

"Don't show him to the girls. He is yours, and yours only. You put him in a good spot, next to your heart. May I suggest you do the same when you travel back home, because the authorities may not want to see him go? So be careful."

Oh, my Lord.

But I did not worry too much. After all, Theo had said that it was given to me with good intent.

All would be well. For sure. Wouldn't it?

"Thank you from the bottom of my heart. For caring. And being my brother."

As Theo had requested, I did not tell the girls about my conversation with him, nor about the little jade man. I sometimes tucked the amulet into my bra to carry him with me. At the end of the day, when I took him out from my left bra cup and held him in my hand, he was the temperature of my skin. Sometimes he seemed to be giving me a cheeky grin. I adored him.

A few years later, I would meet Captain James, who became an exceptional man in my life, but that is a different story. One day I showed James the little Mayan Man, as I needed his help.

"I love holding him, but what I would really like is to wear him around my neck. Until now, I have carried him with me by tucking him into my bra cup, and I would love to find a way to be able to wear him. He has a small hole going through the narrowest part; under is his little face, and above is his body; it's his neck, I guess."

"Let me see," James said.

I gave James the little jade man. He took his leather lace out of his shoe.

"More tricks with the shoelace?" I laughed, recalling the time when he had expertly removed a cork out of a bottle by tying a knot in his shoelace and using it as a lever.

But what was he up to now?

"Can you please pass that glass of brandy you poured for

me?" he asked me as he sat on my coral and muted gold sofa, which I loved so much.

"Sure," I replied.

By that time in my life, I knew him better, and I believed in CJ and in whatever he did.

I watched as he dipped the lace into the brandy. Somehow it made the leather more pliable, and it enabled James to thread it through the hole in the little jade man's neck. James made a sliding knot for me to wear the figurine around my neck. The length of the necklace allowed the figurine to be snuggled between my bosoms. That was the perfect spot for him. You could not see him when I was dressed. But I knew he was there.

And it gave me a centre of gravity that I could not quite explain.

Years later, during our thirty-year Reunion, I brought him with me to show Theo that I still had him. I forgot to take him from around my neck at the pool on the detox day after a relatively heavy night the evening before. It was Bash, who sidled up to me and wanted to know more about the little jade man.

Hélène

"What the hell is going on with you, Hélène? I know you are smoking hot, but you look like you are fuming from what I can see on this Skype screen."

"I know, I am!" Hélène blurted out. "Alvaro makes me erupt! I have been here for three weeks, and still, I have not been able to get him to commit to the upcoming workshops for which we need his property. I need this vineyard. I have already done an olive grove. A vineyard is the next logical location."

"I want to hear all about that, but first, I want to know why there is smoke coming out of your head."

Hélène looked at herself on her laptop to see what I was referring to.

"Oh, that's not me. That is Etna. She seems to be continuously fuming these days. I used to find it spectacular as she erupted beyond the garden. Now I find it boring. My theory is to say what you need to, explode, if necessary, but get back to being less obvious. Mount Etna is in perpetual turbulence. I cannot deny that I am starting to know how that feels. Alvaro is so frustrating. Nonetheless, I believe in blowing your top, making your point, and then moving on to planting seeds in the fertile lava of your erupted soul."

"How poetic, dearest *Helena,* you are on your way to becoming *Truly Italian.*"

"Never, Vivi! These guys are scintillatingly delicious. At the same time, they are unimaginably and frustratingly unpredictable. They are hot and irresistibly attractive. However, in other moments, they are *Mudda Fukkas,* just like every other man on this earth. Same old story, same old song, it goes alright till it goes all wrong. And it has gone all wrong. I need to get out of here, get some space between us. Let him do his wine and olive oil by himself. He sees me as a slave. I am good at marketing, communication, and PR of his products. And he is good at the very same thing, but the product, in this case, is *himself.* He finds new buyers all the time, some blond, some young, some clever, some dumb. And me. He always sells himself to me. Why do I buy it? I ask myself that same question. He is my Achilles heel. I should move away for a while, go on an adventure, do something different. *Ja,* I can tell you, Viv. I am at the end of the *Strada* with this guy. Time to say *Ciao!*"

"Listen. There will be an epic Reunion of Hotel School– it is coming up in six months. I only just heard on the Facebook group today. We should go to the Grand Ole Reunion. Let's do it!"

"*Va bene!*" Hélène said. "Perfect timing. I need to look forward to something positive. We don't often forget, but now, I need to remind myself that I am deliciously divine, creative, competent, and amazing. By that time, I should be well rid of Alvaro, the *stronzo.* That will be a liberation. Imagine seeing everyone again. OMG, it's going to be so awesome! Do you think Alex will be there? Imagine if I see him again? Do you think there will still be snow on the ground so we can go skiing?"

Hélène asked her questions in quick succession, clearly getting excited at the prospect of getting together.

"Not sure, but let's see, six months from now is early March, so we should have some snow though the slopes may be icy. Whether there is skiing or not, knowing you, you will no doubt find some unsuspecting *Reunion Goer* to go sliding with unless it's Alex, of course. He may expect a re-run down your slopes."

"Oh my God, Vivi, you are so brutal. I am still thinking when I should get off Alvaro, and you are already planning a new sleigh ride in the snow for me."

"Let's confirm and make it happen."

"*Ja*. I am in!" Hélène said. "*Top idee,* Viv, great idea."

"I wonder who stayed in touch and who we have forgotten about altogether," Hélène said. "Who are you looking forward to seeing most?"

"For sure, Maddie, Amilcar, and naturally Theo. And I must admit I wouldn't mind seeing Bash again. I know we never had a thing, but he always intrigued me.

"Viv, take it easy with those Arabs. You had a hell of a ride with that General Salim from Oman."

"Hélène, my dear, Salim was a whole different ballgame and a different calibre. You know the story. I did have that thing with Maz in the UAE, and he is an Arab; I'll give you that, but '*All those Arabs*' is an exaggeration. I can't see how a little toying around with Bash could do any harm. I hear he is living in Marbella now. Some other classmates from our year moved there, too. I thought people went there to retire early."

"Viv, listen to yourself. You still sound surprised, but we are all in half a century age bracket now. At fifty people can be considered ripe for early retirement. You and I are *'Early Retirement Ready'*. Just think of it. A crazy thought."

"As we always say, what's in the age anyway? It will be so brilliant to see everyone again."

Reunion Response

I joined the Facebook Reunion group. Before Christmas, I confirmed my attendance. Hélène did the same and enlisted as an Organising Committee Member. She was an event management expert and was also keen to know which people were confirming. She kept me up to date with new bookings and news on people who were planning to attend. Some confirmed immediately. Others booked a tentative space. Communication heated up on messenger and Facebook as time progressed.

Hélène sent me a WhatsApp when she saw that Bash said he was thinking about coming. We asked those who registered or planned to come to send a picture—one photo from thirty years ago as well as a current one. Bash sent a pic of him sitting in his Aston Martin, looking tanned and wealthy from his place in Spain. I remembered him as a boy, but naturally, now I was looking at a fully-fledged man, though recognisable with his blond locks and blue eyes.

Other pictures started coming in from Conchita and Mia in Mexico. Then, there was a message from Amilcar. The image he sent was of him reclining in his hand-carved rocking chair, overlooking his coffee plantation. Wrapped in a blanket, he conveyed his lovely gentle smile though he looked even paler than usual. I recalled our spectacular time at '*Hacienda Sueño en el Cielo*', and I looked forward to the prospect of seeing Amilcar again.

Deyan sent a pic from his private island, and others included their photos too. Hélène sent them straight through to me. It was great to remember all the people with whom we had spent two years of our lives.

Texts about friendship, sun, snow, air, wine, stars, moon, kisses, laughter, and tears started to flow between the Reunion group members.

However, there were also some immediate misunderstandings and opinions on how things should be done. Some mentioned that they wanted formal events and others preferred just easy non-structured chill sessions.

Over the last thirty years the kids that we were had all grown up. Those same people were now successful hotel owners, business drivers, event organisers, textile traders and, art lovers - as Bash called himself.

I, too, had moved up the ranks in hospitality.

Over time I found myself wedged in the tiny top of the power triangle where authoritarian, ass-licking men felt threatened by creative, go-getting women. Whoever was better at foul play was the most likely to gain the space in the golden triangle at the tip of the top. I could not accept the licking up and kicking down culture in the higher levels of the travel industry echelons. I had left to set up my own business.

As a consultant, I engaged in work I enjoyed with reasonable people, with whom you could work effectively and from whom you could detach after the project was complete. I felt that was the way to go. Rather than be tied into politics and problems, this was my new business model - consulting. However, it was not my goal. I wanted to find multiple income streams that allowed me to put my proverbial eggs into various baskets. Ultimately, I was looking to set up a business I enjoyed. People could buy my product online while I was sleeping. I registered my company and several trademarks and started up some businesses, none of which had yet taken off. Until they did, I was committed to continuing my consulting projects, mainly in the Middle East and some in Europe.

I had been trying to find out if Maddie was coming. I wanted to see her again. Ten years ago, I had seen her once just as I was going through my relationship with General Salim. Maddie had lived in Ethiopia for ten years by then and was married to a good-looking, fun-loving, hard-drinking, international fashion model. He was half Spanish, half Ethiopian.

Maddie called him her 'Exquisite Caramelito'.

Maddie said he was an utter stud in the sack.

When I saw Maddie back in the UK, we spent the afternoon together in Kent. Having not been in touch, certainly not regularly, we reconnected straight away. We enjoyed a friendship that did not require monthly maintenance or yearly servicing. I was pretty sure that the upcoming Reunion would bring some of those friendships back to life too.

Typically, reunions are not my thing. I always declined invitations and avoided attending cringeworthy events of people thrown together from primary and secondary school. With some embarrassment, I recalled those slow dances at class parties in our early pubescent years. The boys did not seem to know that deodorant was necessary and appropriate. We had pimples, issues, love interests, and crises. Why celebrate any of that?

Those reunions are most definitely not for me.

However, a Reunion with my *Mountain Mates* was a different ballgame entirely. When we lived and loved on the mountain, we were at the beginning of becoming ourselves. As people, gaining a sense of self, we were still in total turmoil. We were hormonal. The boys were testosterone motivated, and the girls had their challenges to tackle. We were all transitioning and growing up.

I loved that stage in life; it was where I began to understand what it was that made me tick. Development was happening to us all. The bond that grew in the process was unimaginable. And unbreakable, we firmly believed. This Reunion of the years 1983-1988 was one I wanted to attend.

I had not planned to be on the organising committee. Hélène had.

On the 14th of February, Hélène called me from Sicily.

"*Hola chica*," I answered when she rang me via Skype. I recognised her ID. "Happy V day to you. How is Alvaro, the Latin Lover behaving?"

"Forget about that sad excuse of a man. Viv, I need your help," she said.

"What's up, darling?"

"You know I agreed to be on the organising committee of the Reunion?"

"Yes. How is that going? I hope you are seeing some of our dear friends confirming their attendance. Is your blast from the past coming?"

"Yes, he is. And that is the issue. I was working on the registration list and have my laptop open. I went off down the garden to pick up lettuce from the vegetable patch, only to come back to find Alvaro browsing my files. I asked everyone to send in an old photo of themselves at school thirty years ago, as well as one of their current selves. Alex sent in a pic of himself surrounded by his family. And an old one of him and me. He has his arm around my shoulder and is patting my head with his tennis racquet in the shot. He always used to joke with me, and I loved playing tennis with him, as well as most other games," she laughed. "That pic was a great favourite of mine, and it threw me back to those days on *The Mountain of Love*. When Alex sent me the photos, I couldn't help but feel envious of him with his wife and four children, now all grown up. He is a grandfather now, as there is a toddler in the photo, and Alex is holding a baby. So, that is not so great. But after I had seen that attachment, I opened the other one, and there I saw myself. In that picture, taken after the tennis match, thirty years earlier, I looked so happy. I felt the butterflies as if no time had passed. The strange thing that happened was that my heart and soul forgot that life had moved on and everything was now different. Those old memories and first love feelings are hard to erase. Have you ever woken up from a dream and felt deep anger for somebody or deep love? Whatever triggers it, the feeling is real. The image of Alex and me triggered an emotion. I realised at that moment that Alvaro never made me feel like Alex did. I know that I am a middle-aged woman, whatever the hell that means, but my heart has not aged or changed its needs. I need love, appreciation, and good times. My life is no fun anymore, Viv. A part of me has died, and like a lung that doesn't get any oxygen that piece will shrivel up and fall off."

"Wow, that sounds like a bit of a challenging episode. I am so sorry to hear, my dear. That sounds utterly bloody. Tell me, what is Alvaro doing looking at your files?"

"He is Italian with southern blood and a jealousy problem. He boils easily. He was already upset when I told him I was planning on going to the Reunion some weeks back. He gave me the silent treatment and sulked. I had not told him earlier, as I knew he wouldn't like it. I worked on the files, and he decided to dig into what was happening and the plans.

I was looking forward to the event and working towards making it happen, and he didn't like it. He started rooting through my computer files.

When he came across that photo of Alex and me, looking youthful and with a smile on my face, minus my menopause muffin top, Alvaro asked, 'Who is this *Ragazzo*?' I replied that he is Alex, an old boyfriend of mine, from thirty years ago. Alvaro threw his hands up in the air and let out some Italian expletives. He then kicked the table leg so hard that it cracked. As a result, the tabletop sloped, sending my laptop crashing to the floor, followed by the lemons and open olive oil bottle, creating a culinary IT disaster on the rug.

When I dived to retrieve my laptop in a mission not to lose that lovely picture, he kicked the table again, which collapsed entirely and crushed the lemons beneath it. The scene of disruptions infuriated him even more. He told me that he did not want me to go to the Reunion and immediately instructed me to stop my involvement. Then he left the mess he caused for me to clear up, telling me that I am the reason for this collapse, so I am to blame and that he was pretty sure I was planning an affair."

"But it was thirty years ago, and you guys stopped dating in the second year. What the hell is he worried about? Bloody hell Hélène, that is serious."

"Viv, I know it is ridiculous. I told him he was '*patetico*', which he did not like one single bit. But he doesn't like anything I do these days, so his response is the least of my worries. I am concerned about the situation Viv because without seeing Alex and based on his confirmation and message, there is a flame in the deepest of my soul. I feel a glimpse of a flicker, energy so raw, it scares me. If I am honest, I started to think and fantasise about what might happen if I were to see Alex again. Do you follow my drift? I mean, can you imagine when you see Bash? I know you did not consummate your frisson as *Protector Theo* always interfered. God only knows why - but what will happen when you two lock eyes again after all this time?"

"I have no idea. We will have to see," I laughed.

In fairness, the thought had crossed my mind. I wondered how I would respond, but I was not thinking about the eventuality in the same vein that Hélène was.

"What you are saying is understood, but why are you so worried about the memory awakening something in you? We were starting off in our lives all those years ago. Without parents, on the mountain in our new-found mini paradise. We were impressionable. I can recall those memories and experiences at the press of an emotional button. The simplest of triggers can hurtle you back to a moment in time. Wasn't it kind of cool that you had that experience? It must be nice to feel those butterflies, even if there was no love affair going on.

Just enjoy the beauty of feelings and know they are still alive in you."

"That is partly the point, Viv. With Alvaro, I feel nothing anymore. I have decided I want 'out'. I want to re-invite happiness into my life, not necessarily with a man. Oh, that sounded odd. I don't mean with a woman. I like men, but perhaps I should give them a rest and spend some time by myself and get to know *me* again. I need to get away from the erupting and disruptive world where I find myself now. I need to lose Alvaro and Etna and let them spew their sorrows and frustrations without me."

Hélène laughed, though I could sense she was struggling and figuring out what to do next.

"Seems you have reached a point of no return, my dear. That is often a good sign. When clarity prevails, you can move towards a better place. I am here to do whatever I can help with."

"You can help me, Viv. I am begging you to do so. Can you take over my place on the committee? The deadline for registering and payment is on the 29th of February. I had thought I might use this leap year to propose. After all, they only come around every four years. I am now half a century old and have never been married. I try most things once in life, but my proposing to a bloke won't be this year. That's for sure. Maybe it is best to stay single and love yourself first. Rely on yourself only."

"*Chicitita,* first, no problem about the committee stuff. Send me the files and all related information. I shall take care of what is needed. Let me know who the other people on the team are, and I will connect. On a different note, I recommend you wipe all the files from your computer so Alvaro doesn't have his next epic spaghetti combustion fit. Nobody needs that level of drama."

Then I went on to ask, "What is your next move, Hélène?"

"I won't be going to the Reunion, Viv. I need to pack up and move out of here. It is not the time to plan for a trip to Switzerland. I need to return to Amsterdam. Thank goodness I still have my pad and didn't give it up. It's Valentine's day today, and I have never felt so wretched on any V-Day in my life. I can no longer smell the roses. It is time to move on."

We chatted for a bit longer and agreed to organise a mini Reunion for ourselves in the not too distant future. I was sorry Hélène would not attend but pleased that it would not take a Reunion to see her again. I had found her again three years after we had both left school and before she'd moved to Malibu, where she lived with her Beau and two kittens. That relationship had ended up badly. I remembered the heartache and pain she had gone through then. The break-up with Alvaro was perhaps not as dramatic as her previous one, yet it was painful and poignant. It seemed that Hélène had had a realisation because of it. She had to listen to her heart and respect herself. No one could make you feel downtrodden unless you let them.

I recalled my adventures and emotional safaris. I considered them to be valuable journeys. Ones that, in the end, allowed me to develop, to become.

"We will so miss you on *The Mountain*. It won't be the same without you. We will toast you every time we raise our glasses. You know that."

"I know that dearest Viv. It will be great, and I know you will have a blast. I need to regain *terra firma*. We need to

Carpe the *Diem,* my dear. As we said, we are half a century young—time to go at life full blast and with all guns blazing. Let's propel ourselves into the *Era of Erotica, Excellence,* and the next *Diva Decade*! I think Costa Rica may have to be our mini Reunion place. I have woken up and am ready to smell the coffee."

"Agreed, Costa Rica it will be. I will let Amilcar and Theo know. Our perfect Costa Rican hosts."

Pleased that we had planned something to look forward to, I sent Hélène a hug and wished her luck.

"See you soon," I said.

"For another cartoon," she ended my sentence.

We laughed and hung up.

My graduation year was 1986. The committee consisted of Alice, a girl from the class of 1983 and Robert from the class of 1987. The three of us formed a WhatsApp group and coordinated the last registrations, payments, and room assignments for those wanting to stay in the school rooms.

The confirmations came in thick and fast. In a way, it was nice to be part of the committee as I received first-hand information on who was attending, where they were living and what they were doing now. We designed a simple questionnaire asking about the person, the year they graduated, whether they needed accommodation in the school building and whether they wanted a discounted ski pass. Additionally, we asked which events they intended to join, along with the appropriate amount and transfer details.

The Reunion was to take place over three days—a long weekend during early March 2016. On the arrival day, we would manage the check-ins and the distribution of keys. Each attendee would receive an envelope that included food and beverage promotional vouchers for some of the restaurants in the village.

On day one, there would be evening drinks and a welcome dinner. The next day, we planned to go up the mountain for skiing and a day at leisure. At night on the second day, a Swiss Night was scheduled in the canteen, along with a disco. Malcolm, our DJ from thirty years ago, had agreed to spin the vinyl and play our favourites from that era, way back when. On the last day, we planned a mega brunch. With Champagne, mimosas, eggs Benedict and anything you may wish to eat or drink after the main party the night before. Brunch time would start at five in the morning and run until four o'clock in the afternoon, considered the end of the organised activities and the day of departure for most attendees. By offering food from breakfast before dawn, the stalwart party goers who had not made it to bed and had the munchies could enjoy their breakfast. And those Reunion attendees who wanted to have a lie-in after a hard night of partying could wake up at their leisure.

There would be a great representation coming from Latin America, especially Mexico. Johnny from the Dominican Republic had confirmed he would be coming, resulting in an immediate spike in the bookings. Johnny was a natural pull, and we were glad he confirmed his attendance. Hélène had already told me in our Skype conversation that Alex, her ex-beau from the Netherlands, was coming. I was delighted to see that Theo would be flying in from Costa Rica, yet I was sorry that Amilcar could not come. He declined online. I saw messages of regret. I, too, was so sorry that Amilcar would not be able to attend.

The fact that Theo was close to Amilcar, by extension, had created a bond between Amilcar and me. Theo was the oldest of our little group, our inner circle. When needed, it was Theo who would take a stance and take charge. He did it with me sometimes, primarily where Bash was concerned.

Around Amilcar, Theo was always gentle and protective in the most subtle of ways. There was great respect between those two. Theo always waited up for Amilcar, an OK skier, though sometimes he could suddenly lose his energy out on the slopes. Theo invariably would have a bar of chocolate on him in case Amilcar should feel unwell. He then needed an instant energy boost.

When I asked Theo about Amilcar's condition, Theo told me it was probably diabetes. It seemed a plausible explanation at the time. That condition typically includes symptoms of reduced levels of testosterone, resulting in a lack of sex drive. There was perhaps a medical explanation for Amilcar's more docile male presence. Amilcar was Hispanic. Yet unlike Johnny and our fellow male students from the Dominican Republic, Mexico, Chile, and Argentina, Amilcar did not share the same vitality and explosive responses. Neither in terms of expressing joy or frustration nor as it pertained to sexual exploits.

I was sorry that Amilcar could not be at the Reunion, and I sent him a message saying how much we would miss him and asked if he was OK.

He responded the next day, saying:

'Hola querida Vivi, great to hear from you. Sorry, I can't come. My health is not so good, but in my heart, I am well. It would

make me mucho happy to see you. Maybe you will find a way to pass by and see me here, in your Costa Rican Home. Mi casa es su casa. I hope you enjoy your time and remember me to the crazy bunch. Vaya con Dios mi amiga.

Besos, Amilcar xxx.'

While I was happy to hear from him, Amilcar's words felt ominous. It seemed he was telling me somehow that he would not be around. I made a promise in my heart to go and see him as soon as I could. I sent him a note back, precisely saying that.

He replied immediately, with a simple, *xxx.*

Still stunned by Amilcar's message, I saw Lisa's confirmation come through. She was one of our Dutch friends who had been living in Hong Kong. I wondered whether her attendance was *Johnny induced.* Lisa liked to be around the kind of boys who were the centre of attention or whom one of us might fancy. Once she knew a guy who one of us liked she made a beeline for them. She was pretty. Most guys were typically susceptible to her flirtations. That hugely annoyed us girls, in our college days. But Lisa grew out of it when she settled down with her boyfriend Sven, a match that did not please her Jewish mother; She would have preferred *a Joshua.*

Majida's confirmation was followed on the heels of Bash's tentative communication, saying that he planned to be there if it worked out.

I wondered how I would respond if I were to see him.

All these years later, I was intrigued whether I would still be attracted to him. I recalled when Bash told me he could not chat me up as Theo had warned him against trying his luck with me. At the same time, Theo said that I should avoid Bash and that he was dangerous. I think it was funny that I believed Theo back then and that Bash had listened to him, too, respecting Theo's instructions. I was interested to see whether the attraction between us still existed.

Presumably. Not that I was planning to seduce Bash. No way could Theo stop me from doing whatever I wanted to do, nor could he prevent Bash from doing whatever he wanted to do either. I had to admit, he looked attractive from his picture, smiling through the window of his Aston Martin.

Coco and many other people confirmed their places. I had been keeping an eye out for Maddie though she had not yet registered. It had been a while since last we spoke. I so wanted her to be there. I decided to drop her a line.

'Maddie, Vivi here. God, I don't even know where in the world you are. Thank goodness for LinkedIn. It looks like you are still in Africa. I know we have not been in touch, but I wondered whether you plan to come to the 'Life after School Event', the 'Big Reunion'? I would so love to see you if there were any chance you could make it.'

As time passed by and I did not hear back, I gave up on locating Maddie. She was not on Facebook, and I could not think how to contact her. I was delighted when just before the deadline, she replied to my message. After a brief hello, we exchanged our contact details to ease communication.

'Bussi, I am so happy to hear from you.' she wrote. *'I moved back to Europe in September. It has been full-on. Sorry I did not respond earlier. I am separated. I like my new life, and I am super excited to be back in touch. I need to get a charging cable. I have just returned from my February break, and I left it behind. Just like my cheating husband. Good riddance. The divorce is in the pipeline.*

My angels, Eshe and Emmanuelle, are with me. Thank God. I have lots of manifesting to do. I would love to talk. Let me get my charger back, and I will reconnect.

In the meantime, be safe and furious, Your Forever Neighbour, Maddie xxx.

'Fabulous' that meant to say, XXXX - but 'furious' is good too, sometimes. If I can leave my girls with my sister for the weekend, I will be there! Never fear. Talk soon!'

Maddie used to call me *Bussibärchen* when we lived on the mountain, '*Bussi*' for short. After a while, I sometimes called her the same. It was our term of endearment for each other. When she sent me the message, addressing me as '*Bussi*', I realised I never knew what it translated. I checked Google. Having landed on the German page of *Terms of Endearment*, the search result read: 'Bussibärchen, pronounced *BOOSSIH-baer-schen*'. It went on to say that there's no actual translation for this one, but Bussi does mean *kiss*, so it's along the lines of a *cute little kissy bear*. Not a scientific result though a heart-warming interpretation, nonetheless.

I called her, *Bussibärchen*, *Maddiebärchen* or simply *Maddie*.

A decade had passed since we last saw one another. We had not spoken for so long. How ridiculous that you could connect, as we had done in Kent, and then lose touch again. I resolved to take better care of my friends in terms of staying in touch in the future.

I was elated when, later that day, Maddie confirmed she would be attending.

Roomies

On arrival day, people checked in, picked up their keys and settled into their rooms. Some had flown through the night. Even so, most jet-lagged attendees opted to get stuck in straight away and 'start the partying'. We only had three days together, and we all wanted to make the most of it. It was hilarious to see our friends and colleagues from our college days as adults. Somehow, we still saw each other through the lens of youth, through a thirty-year-old prism.

Three decades had passed, and we picked up where we had left off. As simple as that. Those students who still had their old yearbooks had brought them, and they were displayed around the bar for people to enjoy. They triggered memories of the good old days. New arrivals keep trickling in during the late afternoon though it was less busy by then.

Coco arrived on the arm of a Silver Fox. Having hugged each other like young milkmaids screaming our heads off, I turned my attention to the man by Coco's side. He was tanned and fit, around our age.

"Hi, I am Vivika. I oversee check-in. Can I take your name?"

Coco looked on, smiling.

"I am Reinard," he said, "I am with Colette."

I looked at Coco.

"That's me," she laughed.

"I decided that I should go by my full first name, but no worries, I still respond to Coco. To be fair, when people call me Colette, I don't know who they are addressing until I remember that I changed my name. I will get used to it eventually. You like it, Reinard, because you think '*Colette et Reinard*' sounds better than '*Reinard et Coco*' like you are some cradle snatcher." She laughed heartily.

Reinard bent down to plant a kiss on her head. She put her arm around his middle and smiled back up at him, her green eyes ablaze.

"Update me, Coco, my dear, or Colette, I mean. I have been calling you Coco for the past four decades. Sorry, it will take some getting used to using your new name. It will be a tricky habit to shake!"

"Forget it, Viv; Colette is not going to stick. Coco is fine. And as for Reinard here, he won't be requiring a separate room."

She dangled her key with a massive metal keyring with the room number engraved on it.

"I already checked in, and Reinard is my man for the weekend. He will be staying with me. Although he didn't attend our school, he knows the mountain and the students better than any of us. Reinard came here in the last year we were here. He has been a '*Moniteur du ski*' for thirty years now, so he has seen some comings and goings. And this weekend, he will see some more. I met him in *Le Pâtisserie* on the way up. I could not drive by without picking up a delectable *Quiche Lorraine* for one. Reinard spotted me, and we hit it off again straight away. He hadn't forgotten me."

Coco winked at Reinard and pulled his face down until she could reach up to kiss him. Reinard was not particularly tall, but next to Coco, he was like Theo is, to me, much taller.

"After I had eaten my quiche for one, Reinard invited me to what he remembered was my favourite ice cream for two. We shared a celebratory '*Coupe Tête à Tête*', laden with cookies, Smarties, cream and two Balistos popping out of the middle of the fruit-bowl sized treat. I think it was a prelude to the sweetness I will indulge in over the next few days. It may seem like I just picked Reinard up as I was going up the mountain, but we have history. And history repeats itself." She smiled again.

Suddenly, it clicked. "Oh my God, this is '*The Reinard; Red-Ribbon Reinard*', the new ski teacher at the time whom you had set your sights on!"

"The very one, my dear. '*Reinard the Fox*' is joining me, his foxy lady, this weekend. We shall meet up later when we make it out from our den, if indeed we do."

Reinard stooped to pat Coco on the bum, and then he took her hand. Off they strolled, Coco and the Fox.

I met some other people from the previous and subsequent years. Some of them I had bumped into during skiing holidays when they too were revisiting their old stomping ground. Then Neil, our beloved computer teacher, rocked up with his partner, the lovely Caroline. They had been together for twenty-five years, though they had never got around to getting married.

Neil pulled me to one side and said, "Vivika, you are the first to know. I am going to pop the question to Caroline during the Reunion. Can you give me a late check-out on departure day?

I have something special planned for her. It involves a balloon ride, starting in Chateaux d'Oex."

"Oh Neil, how brilliant! I am thrilled for you. So happy to see you and delighted it wasn't sergeant-major Neuhaus who confirmed. That might have ruined our fun."

"Lucky for us both," he laughed. His dimples were still intact and even more pronounced on his matured face. "Neuhaus used to give me a hard time too. He could not take me seriously as a teacher. I am competent enough, but I was only five years older than most of the students, which did not sit well with him. Anyway, I am older now," he laughed.

"Aren't we all," I grinned. "Brilliant to see you."

I went to get a coffee from the kitchenette. Alice from the organising committee was completing a check-in.

As I walked back to the registration area, I realised from her posture, that it was Maddie.

I placed my coffee next to the nearest plant pot as I knew it would spill when I hugged her. The paper cup toppled over onto the floor.

I will deal with the spill later, I thought.

"Mad Maddie!" I called out.

She turned as I ran towards her. "Bussi! Oh my God! Who would have thought this was going to happen? I didn't know if I could make it until the last minute, but my sister came up trumps, and she's looking after the girls! I know they are almost grown-up, but I didn't want to leave them home alone. Not just yet anyway."

"I am so happy!"

We hugged and then stood back from each other, laughing but with tears in our eyes.

"I booked your old room for you. And mine for me. We will be neighbours again over this long weekend. I cannot wait to catch up!"

"Me too, Bussibärchen. Such utter bliss to be on our mountaintop! I can't wait to see everyone we know and most of all, you."

"The feeling is entirely mutual, Mads. Here is your key. You know the way."

"See you in the bar, I presume?"

"If we are ready at the same time, we can come over to the main building together."

"Sounds perfect. I will give you a knock or a kick on the door, Buss, when I am ready. Otherwise, just pound on mine, and we will be *bar-bound* together."

Just as Maddie was about to go to her room, Majida, Lisa, and Theo arrived simultaneously.

"Oh Lordie, how lovely. Three in one!"

We hugged and agreed to meet in the bar later.

Alex was yet to appear, but Alice said she had received a call from him saying he was on his way. He needed a bit more time as his flight was late in arriving.

Bash was a law unto himself and would rock up whenever he was ready. I hoped he would come soon, though I would have preferred to know when. That way I could make sure I would greet him with a drink in my hand.

Reconnected

Maddie knocked on my door in the Annex. "Ready, Buss?" she asked through the door.

"Yup, just a tick, will be right there," I shouted back.

It was great to be neighbours again. We locked arms and made our way over to the main building where the bar was situated. It was heaving. People were having evening cocktails, though some had their first after breakfast and never moved from their couch in the bar's lounge area.

I looked in through the glass that separated the wide sanatorium corridor from the bar. Theo was there with Majida, Coco and Lisa. Maddie and I ordered a drink and went over to our group of friends.

"*Hola chicas calientes*, you look too hot to trot," Theo said. "Now, how are we boys going to be able to leave you alone this evening without getting into trouble?"

Theo put his arm loosely around Maddie's shoulders as he raised his beer bottle to toast with her wine glass. At that point, Bash arrived.

He made it.

Drink in hand with that broad captivating smile of his, he joined our group and hugged us all, holding me a bit longer than the others, or so it seemed.

Bash raised his glass to everyone and then touched glasses with me, saying, "Vivikaaaaah! It is about time we meet again. I can't wait to catch up and spend some proper time with you."

I shot Theo a look, who was happily chatting to Maddie. I relaxed and settled into what I hoped would be a stress-free evening and a lot of fun.

Then Alex made an appearance, a glass of whiskey in hand. We all welcomed him and hugged each other all over again. Soon he asked where Hélène was.

"I was expecting her to be here," he said. "It is one of the greatest things I was looking forward to, to see her again and to get reacquainted. She is a fabulous girl."

"She wasn't able to make it, unfortunately, because she has some matters to sort out. She mentioned the picture you sent of your lovely family. I hope they are well?"

Alex took a sip of his whiskey, "All is more manageable now, Viv. It has been a difficult decade. After I met Hélène, I often thought about her. We used to have such great times together. I heard through the grapevine that she was living with a guy in Malibu, so I did not pursue her any further. I closed that chapter. Years later, I met a woman called Clarissa, who may not have been the love of my life, but we got on well together and enjoyed each other's company. We had three lovely children. They are all grown up now, and my son has two kids of his own. The picture I sent in was of happier times when my wife, three children, daughter-in-law, and kids visited our house. I had arranged for a photographer to take a picture of all of us together. I knew I needed to capture our family one last time while I still could. My wife suffered from a rare disease which we found out about just before our second grandson was born. My wife was determined to look her grandson in the eye but died a few weeks later. And as she closed her eyes, she looked into mine one last time."

"Oh Alex, I am so deeply sorry for your loss."

I took hold of his hand and walked him out of the busy bar onto one of the half-moon shaped balconies that jutted out from the bar area. The vantage point overlooked the mountains beyond and the sports centre in the distance. As we stepped outside, I hugged him. He put his arms around me. His broad shoulders started to shake as he began to cry. He tried to hold his pain back, as so many men do.

"I am sorry," he whispered. "It was two years ago now; I thought I was over it. But I guess you never get over the loss of a loved one. Even though my wife was not the love of my love like Hélène was, I cared for her deeply. She gave birth to my children, and we became the best of friends. I have not cried since the day she passed. I thought I was OK. I am not."

"You will be Alex," I said softly. "You are with your family. We go way back, and we go way forward together. You did the right thing to come. We are so happy you are with us. When I spoke to Hélène on Valentine's day, of all days, she told me she could not attend the Reunion. She was moving back to Amsterdam from Sicily, or *Silly-Silly,* as she called it after the turmoil with her ex-man."

"Her ex?" Alex looked up as he asked the question.

"Yes, I will leave it to Hélène to share her story if she wants to, but I can tell you, Alex, she always mentions you as being her first love. She compared everyone to you. Hélène said that her times with you were fun, genuine, and full of initiative and possibility. She wondered why it ever finished."

"Really? I would have been so delighted to have seen her. Whatever may or may not have happened. She, too, was my first true love. I think my only one."

"Let us enjoy our time here together in the present moment. Hélène and I are planning a little post-Reunion in Costa Rica. We have not discussed it with Amilcar and Theo yet, or anyone else. You are the first to know."

A gentle smile appeared on Alex's face, "Thank you, Vivi, for your warmth and understanding. And your astute words that we shared our past and, God willing, we still have a future. As well as today."

"That's the Alex I know and love."

Bash joined us on the balcony. After a while, Alex excused himself and went back inside. I started to chat with Bash.

"What do you do, Bash?" I asked him.

"You are not the first one who wants to know. People often ask me that question. I sometimes even ask myself. Let's just say I do all sorts and nothing. I go where the energy and the opportunity take me. Right now, I am being pulled in a particular direction. In *your* direction if you have not yet noticed."

After a while, Alex came back out and said, "Dinner is served, you two."

"I agree for you to sit next to Viv, Alex. But I am sitting on her right. It's Cheese Fondue night. And you know what that means," Bash laughed as we joined the gathered crowd and moved towards the canteen where we used to eat our breakfasts, lunches and dinners. It was also the place where we celebrated national nights.

That night, the theme, predictably, was called 'All Things Swiss'.

Flags adorned the walls, cowbells rang, chocolate fountains were on standby to be reeled in after the cheese fondue. Crates of local white wine had been chilled, and fresh tea was placed on each table. We knew from experience that you should avoid drinking cold water with cheese fondue as it formed a ball in your stomach and could create an upset. For some reason, cold white wine did not have the same bad name as it related to the delicious hot bubbling pot of cheese before me. Not much tea was drunk at dinner. Instead, we relied on a few shots of *Schnapps* to do the trick to aid digestion.

Along with the booze in the cheese fondue and the Schnapps, we had quite a bit of alcohol over dinner.

Bash made sure that I sat on his right. Alex flanked me on the other side. There is a tradition that when you put your bread on your fondue fork, you place it in the bubbling melted cheese and make the sign of the Swiss flag on the cheese, a cross. If you lose your bread, having dipped it into the delicious concoction of Emmental and Gruyere, kirsch, and white wine, you must kiss the person on your right. And I was on Bash's right during dinner.

Bash lost his bread for the umpteenth time. The more he kissed me, the closer he came to my mouth, until he kissed me full on the lips. I played along and gave him a little kiss back.

The whole table shouted, "Wedding, wedding, we want a Reunion wedding!"

It was fun. However, Theo didn't seem to think so.

The Morning After

I was out on my balcony, breathing in the morning air and enjoying the incredible scenery, which I never took for granted. It was God's creation at its best. I heard my dear neighbour pushing open her door to take in the view and the air. Popping my head around the frosted glass dividing our balconies, I greeted her.

"Hi Maddie, good morning. How are you?"

"I am great, Viv. I hope you slept well too. That was a hell of a cheese fondue last night."

"Yes, I'm still recovering but happy we had that Schnapps. It made all the difference. Not a ball in my stomach. A great start to a new day on this glorious mountain."

"I hope we get some proper time to chat," Maddie said. "It was hilariously good fun last night. I had a riot, dancing to those old hits in our good old disco. It was fabulous, but not the best place to talk."

"I agree. Excellent night, but chatting was impossible. Why don't we grab a coffee and catch up? There is an unoccupied room booked for Kim, but unfortunately, he couldn't make it.

We can sneak into it, take the mattresses onto the epic balcony there, and recover from last night. The sun is out too, and I would be so happy to spend some one on one quality time, away from the madding crowd. What do you think?"

"Ah, bliss, Viv. I cannot think of anything better. We can spend the morning together, then catch up with the others later. I think the pool and the sauna have been booked at *La Résidence* so we can hike down the road to meet the others there afterwards."

"Excellent. How about you pick up the coffees, and I'll pick up the key, and I will meet you in front of room 111 on the first floor, opposite the elevator."

"That is Bash's old room," Maddie remembered.

"I know. I enjoyed sitting next to Bash during the cheese fondue yesterday. He was flirting outrageously, but Theo kept glancing at him. I thought we had gotten over that. We've moved on three decades, for goodness' sake!"

Maddie burst out laughing.

"I noticed," she said. "It seemed to me that Bash kissed you multiple times on the pretext of losing his bread in the melted cheese."

"I know. That blond Arab is a charmer. One to be watched, though not as closely as Theo does," I laughed. "If you get our coffees from the bar, I will fix the place up so that we are comfortable and won't get disturbed. I know that if we stay in our old rooms, they will come knocking. If we hide out in room 111, they will have no idea where we are. I love seeing everyone, but now I need to know all about you."

"Happy with the plan. I will get the caffeine. Double shots. Do you still just like a dash of milk in your coffee?"

"Yes, please, Mads. Just a dash."

I went up to room 111 and arranged the mattresses on the vast balconies. The sun was warm, and the view of *Les Dents du Midi* was spectacular. Maddie arrived with the coffees. She settled into her story and why she moved back to Germany, having spent twenty years in Africa. A place she had got to know and love.

"I will take you on my emotional safari," she said. "Climb aboard for a bit of a jerky ride. I am afraid there is a chunk of history I need to offload on you, and it is rather one man-centric."

"I want to hear your story. As much as you want to tell me."

Maddie gulped her coffee and started.

"I met Manu in Marbella, where I was attending an art fair. My employer, a hotel owner, knew I loved art. He sent me on a mission to procure pieces for the new top luxury hotel in Addis. Directors and CEOs of Sotheby's, Saatchi & Saatchi, and royalty and artists attended the event. I was looking forward to the occasion. I stayed in the place where the art exhibition and auction were taking place. It was a super over the top hotel overlooking the Med. Manu represented a well-known, very upscale fashion label, which shall remain nameless in view of the scandalous context.

The target market at the event was the precise audience that Fashion House X wished to attract. They paid a small fortune to present their new *haute-couture* and dressed Manu in ever-changing outfits as he charmed and mingled with the buyers. The idea was to give pulse and pleasure to the collection, allowing potential buyers to touch the goods. The high-society art lovers appreciated the finest things in life, and Manu hit the mark. His arrogance grew with every event, as did his income. Most women, as well as many men, would make a beeline for Manu. Being at liberty to touch this exquisite creature of a man under the pretext of what he was wearing was tempting. With his delicious caramel skin and tiger coloured eyes, Manu was a seduction so sweet not many could resist. There was only one Manu among many buyers. He was used to being desired and became incredibly conceited. He was *hautain en Haute-couture.*"

Maddie continued to recount events. While in Marbella, Manu had not managed to engage Maddie. She was tied up, and no matter how he tried, she didn't look at him. She was the only person in the room who paid no attention to him. Manu noticed Maddie passing her business card to a very camp and renowned artist. After some time, she said her farewell to the older gentlemen and moved away towards the exit. Manu followed her, and in the lobby of the luxury hotel, he saw her disappear in the elevator. Manu went back inside and struck up a conversation with the artist Maddie had exchanged business cards with. The artist introduced himself as Jacques, and he was *très content* to meet Manu. The seventy-year-old talented man may have thought he was presented with a new canvas to let his creative powers loose on. But Manu was not interested. He had only one goal in mind. Maddie tells the story as Manu had told it to her, from Manu's perspective.

"The girl you were just talking to, who was she? I think she was a long lost friend, but I could not get to her on time to say hi. It would be amazing if it were her. I am not interested in her, but it was a crazy coincidence if she was in town. I should like to say hello."

The tactical mention that Manu was not interested in the girl appeared to please Jacques.

"I will tell you all about my conversation with your friend but allow me to do so over dinner. I may be in my seventies, but I am ready to feast my eyes on the beauty of you. It has been three years since my darling Charles passed away, and I am quite sure he was fed up with me not indulging in a bit of masculine magnificence. I realise now I have missed the candy store, so I kept myself to myself, and the only elongated tools I hold in my hands are paintbrushes. I may express myself using them, but that is not the same as feeling the warmth and the pulse of the blood flowing through your veins. I want to able to look into the eyes of my fellow artist in love, as we create *'le feu d'artifice'*, and merge in a joyous explosion."

Realising that Jacques was looking for a cock-tale, Manu later told Maddie, he could not wait to make his escape. But he wanted the name and number of the dismissive girl.

With his charming smile, as Manu told Maddie, he turned to Jacques and softly said, "I am sorry for your loss. Three years means nothing in a lifetime of grief. It will be my pleasure to accompany you this evening." It was left unclear whether dinner would also have dessert on the menu.

Later, it transpired that as soon as Manu persuaded Jacques to pass him Maddie's business card, he exclaimed, "My God, it was her. Maddie was here. I can't believe it. What a small world."

Of course, Manu had never met Maddie before he read her name on the business card. Now he not only knew her name but her contact details too. Manu proceeded to take a photo for his reference. Although she was European, her address on the card said she worked in Addis. His hometown!

Having accomplished his mission, Manu excused himself to Jacques and said he would be right back.

Maddie had picked up some work she needed to complete and had taken a seat in the lobby. She saw Manu, the model, go up to reception and hand the receptionist a note. He did not notice her and went back into the restaurant. Only to return ten minutes later, punching the air. The scheming Manu had told reception to let him go back into the restaurant and then call him. The receptionist followed the instruction. When Manu received the call, he made up an excuse to Jacques, saying he was urgently needed and left. Jacques was left to swallow his sole meunière alone.

Still sitting in the lobby, Maddie received a phone call on her mobile. It was Manu.

Maddie told how Manu somehow managed to link the art, which Maddie had admired, and said he wanted to buy some pieces. Manu said he would like a second, informed opinion from Maddie before purchasing the artwork. And could they meet up? Maddie considered Manu's request. She loved art, and so Maddie agreed to a meeting. She told Manu it would have to be over breakfast the next day, as she was flying out at lunchtime."

Maddie and Manu met in the lobby of the hotel and introduced themselves formally. They walked into the same restaurant where Manu had obtained Maddie's details the night before, achieved by pretending to Jacques that he already knew Maddie.

As Maddie and Manu entered, the waiter greeted them and

asked for their room numbers, which they gave.

"If only I had known you were in that room last night, I might have knocked on your door," Manu flirted, but he quickly recoiled when Maddie looked at him. He continued quickly, "Sorry, that was not a good start to meeting you."

"No, it was not. If you are planning on cheap conversation, I see no reason to sit down. If, on the other hand, you would like to discuss art, as you said, then please be my guest."

"You will be my guest, of course," Manu replied.

"No, thank you. We can agree to split the bill if you would rather. I don't like to be indebted to anyone or send the wrong message. And based on your earlier comment, perhaps I need to be very clear. Let us sit by the window rather than out on the terrace. Though the sun is shining, there is a chill coming off the Med this morning."

A waiter served coffee. Then Maddie's face broke into a charming smile, full of warmth and welcome. Manu thought he had redeemed his place until he realised Maddie's smile had absolutely nothing to do with him.

"Jacques," she said.

Manu choked on his coffee. He had not seen Jacques coming towards them as he was facing the other way from the entrance. Jacques stood behind Manu and offered him a linen napkin to clear up the coffee that had landed on the crisp white tablecloth.

"Thank you," Manu muttered, his skin turning an interesting shade from its usual rich, deep tanned, olive colour. With the blood rushing to his cheeks, his colour of shame may have been called aubergine.

Maddie noticed something was off, though she did not let on.

"So, you have found each other. How wonderful to see!

I am glad I could be of help. Don't let me keep you. You must have much to catch up on. I will leave you to it. I will be shipping your paintings Mademoiselle Maddie or was it, Madame?"

Maddie didn't clarify her status. Instead, she said, "Jacques, you are most welcome to join us. I am sure Mr Manu too would be delighted, would you not Mr Manu?"

She watched his unease increase as he sat across the table from her. Jacques thanked Maddie, elegantly declining her kind invitation.

"I must get my easel out and paint this magnificent view. It is crisp and clear, and my creative juices are pulsating." Jacques shot Manu a flirtatious look, embraced Maddie and excused himself.

"Interesting start to the day, Mr Manu, don't you agree? Perhaps you would care to explain what is going on. My initial take on matters is that you play with reality, or I am mistaken, Mr Manu? You have my number, but I don't think I want yours. As a matter of interest, how did you obtain it? And allow me to interject that if you feel you should lie about that too, you may simply leave."

Manu moved uneasily in his seat. He looked like he was about to say something when it appeared Manu did a mental readjustment on what he was about to say.

"You caught my eye, but you had no interest in me. You were the only one in the room who did not look at me. And I wanted to find out about you."

"Ah, a challenge. I see. I am dealing with the basics here. What a pity. But never mind, let us have breakfast and say goodbye. I do need a bite before I leave, so please, if you don't mind, pass me the butter."

"I am ashamed. And sorry. Please forgive me. I very much wanted to speak with you. I understand now that what I saw as being resourceful was not right. I lied to Jacques to get your number. I saw you speaking to him as you passed him what looked like your business card. I abused the situation and eventually got what I was after, but not in the right way."

"What are you after, Mr Manu, if I may enquire?"

Maddie caught Manu off guard. In that split second, Maddie confided in me; she saw a shadow of a boy, something tender, unadulterated. Maddie was a compassionate and intuitive person. Something had shown up on her sensitivity radar which in retrospect may have led her to collision with a psychologically disturbing iceberg. Manu had not made a good initial impression, but Maddie's gut had picked up on a *glimpse of something real.* She was attracted to authenticity, both in art and people. She typically listened to her gut. However, Manu seemed like an arrogant oddball, albeit a stunning one. She could not but benefit from her doubt.

"Let us put the events behind us and start again, Mr Manu. I presume that is your real name?"

Seemingly relieved at having been given a chance, Manu said, "Manu is my nickname. My real name is Emmanuel. Manu for short." He paused. Then, in a softer voice, he said, "My mother told me Emmanuel meant *'God is with us'.* She was a most extraordinary woman. Strong, loving and kind. Now she is with God."

He dropped his gaze and looked at his plate. "May God keep her in internal peace."

"I am sorry to hear that. May God keep her."

Manu looked up again, regained his poise, yet didn't speak.

To lift the silence, Maddie asked, "How many siblings do you have, Manu?"

"I used to have seven, but the twins died. They were the youngest. I don't know what happened exactly. After that, my father left. Back to Spain."

"That sounds like a tragic time in your life. I am sorry to hear that. How did your mother cope after your father left and the passing of the twins, if I may ask?"

"My mother went into decline, and we slid into bad times. I never understood what happened. But I was now the man of the house. At the age of 16, I had to step up and take care of my mother and brothers and sisters. I did not know where to start. Soon I found myself associated with traders of art and sellers of drugs. I was young and easy on the eye. They used me to traffic their goods. My mother had no idea."

He paused again. Maddie told me she sensed that he had let on too much about himself. He had lapsed into a moment of unexpected information sharing that perhaps was inappropriate so soon into the conversation. Maddie continued to tell me about the time she first spoke with Manu.

"Ms Maddie, you said you have a lunchtime flight to catch?"

"Yes, I do. I am booked back to Addis via Madrid."

"I would like to change my reservation and come back with you if you are flying Ethiopian Airways."

"I am, and if you can change your ticket, I am OK with that. It seems there are some worthwhile things to talk about."

After breakfast, Maddie and Manu checked out and set off to the airport. It took some time to fly back to Addis. The two of them talked about all sorts. Manu felt amazed that someone could be interested in him as a man rather than his exterior shell. During the flight, somewhere over The Mediterranean, Manu resorted to what he knew best. Flirting.

Maddie calmly looked at him and said, "If you and I are going to be friends, then you need to be Manu, the Man rather than Manu, the Model."

And with that, they sealed the start of their relationship.

Maddie's Man

Manu changed. Maddie warmed to him. They hung out. They talked, laughed, and connected. As they were both in Addis, they spent time together and increasingly their bond grew. Manu felt more comfortable showing his vulnerable side, though more so when he drank and smoked joints. At those times he shared his past experiences more easily.

Maddie looked at me with her huge brown Liza Minelli eyes, "I know you were never into weed Viv, even though you are half Dutch. But I see smoking a joint, if you inhale deeply, as if you are bringing the magic of the plant into your soul, allowing internal boundaries to melt away and to be one with the cosmos."

She was ethereal, my friend Maddie. Some would say a touch eccentric. To me, she was individual and unique.

Maddie continued. "Eventually there was no going back. Manu and I merged and were pretty much joined at the hip. Months later we got married in a simple ceremony. I kept on working up until I fell pregnant with the twins. Manu and I were ecstatic.

"Often twins skip a generation, but maybe my parents' twins that died came back through us. It is perfectly possible, you know, Maddie."

"I know, Manu. I feel that too. We will give them a chance this time. To be loved and to live a full life."

Maddie told me that when the little girls, Emmanuelle and Eshe were born, Manu was awesome. He took the leading role in the household, allowing Maddie to continue her work. When he had modelling assignments, they shared the responsibility. Whenever Manu had to travel, they found a way to work it out.

Maddie continued with her story, "Over the years, however, as the twins grew up, Manu became disengaged. He seemed to be spending more time online than with his daughters and seemed less happy and more distant and silent. And while I prefer people who whisper rather than shout, his silence killed me. I reckon this was the time where you and I lost touch, Bussi."

"Maddibärchen, do you remember the time we met up after the Christmas break, after our first year here?"

Maddie took a sip of her coffee, now no longer hot. She looked at me, her eyes quizzical yet amused, as she intuitively felt some impromptu anecdote was coming on, which she said was one of my hallmarks.

"Do you remember going through the French part of Geneva airport during the first year on our return trip to school after our Christmas break? I met you on arrival, so we could travel back to college together by train and catch up."

"Oh yes, I do. Really well. You cracked me up wearing your Father Christmas hat with that massive green and red pompom and all those little bells sewn onto it. The noise that creation made was the reason I turned round, as you jingle-belled towards me."

"I know Christmas was over but it was a spectacularly awesome hat, so I decided to bring it over to entertain you and to keep my ears warm on the slopes. Like a puppy should not just be for Christmas, neither should a great hat be."

"Why did you stop me from telling you about my man for the sake of a hat?" Maddie laughed.

"Ah sorry. I interrupted you as you referred to preferring people who whisper, rather than shout. Though I don't know why we are such good friends, as you must admit, I am not exactly softly spoken."

"You doughnut Viv. You can be as loud as you like, you are my rock, my mountain range and my favourite neighbour of all times, but I am still not clear on why you told me to stop telling you about Manu."

"Darling Maddie. Do you remember when we met each other before passing through customs? We were on the people mover at the airport as we made our way towards the passport check area. Standing in our spot, chatting away on the horizontal people mover in Geneva airport, all the advertising was related to timepieces and banking. The billboard that stood out, read: '*Money talks. Wealth whispers.*'

Had we been walking; we would have stopped in our tracks. Do you remember we both read the huge letters at the same time and glanced at each other and you, Mads, whispered, '*Now that is class; Subtle, not in your face, genuine and hard to come by.*'"

"I remember," Maddie replied. "And I recall that you said,

'If we ever get into a joint business Maddie, let's remember that slogan and use it.'"

"I remember, especially when you said, you would apply the principle to more than business. You added that you aimed to find a man that lived up to the slogan, but that you were not in a hurry as finding such a jewel, may be down some African mine waiting to be found."

"Bloody hell Bussi, what a great memory. I guess I did not quite live up to polishing my rough diamond from Africa, much as I wanted him to shine," Maddie said.

Enough was Enough

After matters at home got out of control, Maddie confronted Manu and asked him what was up. The first few years he managed to fob her off and avoided being drawn into the subject. Now, Maddie pleaded with him, asking Manu what was going on and questioned why he seemed so disengaged and so deeply unhappy. She softly asked him why he was drinking so much and overdosing on drugs. The answer Manu gave her, as Maddie told me, was stunning and profoundly sad.

"I sat in front of Manu, Vivi. You should have seen it. He used to be such a figure of a man, but on this day his eyes stared aimlessly at the glass of whiskey in his hands. 'What is up, Manu,' I encouraged him. 'You can share anything with me. It's OK. Let me understand.'"

Manu had looked up and locked his dark brown eyes onto Maddie's and said, "I am scared."

"Scared?" Maddie probed.

Whether it was for sales purposes or in personal and tricky situations, we had all been taught that if you genuinely want to know, dig deeper. Probe. But more importantly, listen.

Especially to what was not being said.

Maddie stayed silent until Manu spoke. She said she had an ominous feeling in her stomach but cared about this man.

"Maddie, happiness is temporary. I know that much," Manu had said. "If you think you have the beginnings of something good, it will be taken away. That is how life is. Always."

Maddie was mortified to hear these words from her husband, yet she needed to understand.

"Tell me more," she said, trying not to remember her sales course where we had all learnt this little one liner. Even if you used it in the right way because you cared, it still somehow felt prescribed and not genuine.

"Happiness never lasts. I cannot have it taken away from me again. I know the end is coming. I know that from experience. I don't think I can take more suffering and loss. My mother has been visiting in my dreams saying soothing words and hugging me from heaven. My father too is coming into my thoughts at night, though he comes in the form of nightmares. He says I am like him. And that the twins that he lost and who came to us, will haunt me. I am seeing bad signs ahead. When I go into the street, I see people who give me the look, the evil eye. I have been stopped by people whom I don't know, who tell me that being with a foreigner will mean my downfall. I am Ethiopian, even if I have Spanish blood. I am being glared at. I know that disaster is coming and I am scared. I love you and the girls but I have realised it was my fate to taste happiness but not to savour it. Rather than anyone taking it from me I will be prepared. When my father walked out, I didn't know why. When the twins died, I didn't understand. When my mother left me, it was too soon. When I met you, I thought everything would be different. You saw me for a man, rather than a model. You peeked into my soul and embraced me. But it seems my soul is black, contaminated, broken, and rotting. I have now experienced the feeling of ecstasy, of being loved by someone else other than my late mother. I experienced a sense of purpose which I felt when the twins were born. Being able to look after them and you felt good. Because it was not out of desperation or need, like it was with my siblings. It was done out of choice.

But now I have been warned by the evil powers. And I will not wait for them to get me, to taunt me and hurt you. I will not let it happen. Maybe the twins are not the angels we thought, but the re-embodied spirits of the ones who left and have returned."

He looked out of the window as if in a trance.

Maddie told me she had been flabbergasted and horrified at the outpouring of dark thoughts. She knew that in all cases, you should stay quiet. With her heart beating in her throat, she went over to where Manu was sitting. She took his hands in hers and sat down on her knees in front of him, with her head bowed into his lap. His hands felt cold, limp almost, and the energy they normally had which was electric, had gone. It was as if Manu had died even though he was alive and right there in front of her. She knew his exit from her life was coming; The process of decay had set in.

Surely there was no such thing as an evil eye.

Manu seemed to be raking up the pain of his past and believed it was his destiny to be tormented. That even though he had felt love and happiness, it could not prevail. This time, he said, he would pre-empt the inevitable and take matters into his own hands. He would anticipate darkness and take control by destroying the very blessings that had been bestowed upon him.

The love of a woman and the adoring hearts of his little girls.

Maddie had tried to be there, offering support, love, understanding and patience, but it seemed Manu's mental position was set. Manu increased his drinking, as well as his habit of smoking pot. He used to light up in the evening; now he smoked in the mornings too before the girls went to school, Maddie would catch the scent of ganja coming from the garden. No doubt there was a harder substance involved.

It was as if Manu was trying to speed up his self-prophesy and fall into an abyss. He was aiming for auto-destruction.

It was the most wretched time. Even though Maddie's heart, so full of love, had spotted the cracks in Manu's soul correctly, she could not fix him. It was too late. The looming iceberg under the troubled waters of his soul, had broken their journey through life as a family. The vessel of their marriage was about to hit the rocks.

Manu was too far gone. He increased his reliance on drink and drugs.

When Manu travelled for his modelling gigs, he used to sleep around and not be in touch. Matters became worse as he grew more aggressive. Maddie loved him, but although she, personally might be able to cope, she could not risk Eshe and Emmanuelle being hurt, and guarded them like a lioness.

One evening Manu, completely drunk and stoned out of his mind, wanted to wake his sleeping teenage girls to play marbles in the sand behind the house. It was a random, odd, inappropriate, and scary situation. Maddie's Man had lost the plot. She tried to reason with him, yet when Manu insisted on waking the sleeping youngsters in the depth of night, Maddie stood in front of their bedroom door, pleading with him. He pulled her by her sweater towards him and then flung her backwards, resulting in her head being slammed into the door of the girls' bedroom. Her head ricocheted off the door as he let her go and she slumped to the floor. Emmanuelle and Eshe woke up and started screaming. Maddie was bleeding. Bruised and battered, with her head spinning, she pulled herself up and opened the bedroom door. The girls, who shared a room, ran to Maddie who hugged them in the dark, dripping blood onto their pyjamas, until they pushed the two single beds together to barricade the bedroom door. With Maddie in the middle, her twins hung on to her, until they finally fell asleep. Maddie did not. She guarded her precious loves all night.

At dawn, as the sun's rays poured in over the windowsill, Maddie got up. She had not slept a wink as she pondered what to do. She was in much pain, both emotionally and physically. The blood had dried up on her skin and clothes and on the girls' pyjamas. Maddie showered, ran the bath for the girls and put her blood streaked clothes into the washing machine. She wondered whether the stains would come out. She told me she didn't know where to turn. The only person she felt would not judge her, and who would understand her and truly care, would be me. She had thought of finding me and calling, but what to say? '*Hi Bussi, I am in trouble. I need you.*'

"Yes, Maddiebärchen, you should have. I will always be here for you and your girls, as I know you will be there for me, my darling neighbour, Sister of my Soul."

We just cried and hugged for a while. Then we talked more.

Maddie told me everything. She explained she could not turn to her family. They all thought she was odd. They did not understand why anyone would ever want to go and live in Africa in the first place. They had never seen the twins; they had not ever visited their home. She had a loving family but Maddie has an X-factor quality they did not understand. Consequently, Maddie could not turn to her family in her hour of need and pain.

The months that followed were horrific for Maddie. She never knew when Manu would rock up and make up. His lovemaking was stratospheric, Maddie would say. Powerful and sensual. When they lay in each other's arms after sex, Maddie felt things would be OK again.

Surely if he could make love to her like that, it was evidence of his ability to be able to feel, and allow himself the light, the oxygen, and the happiness, which all God's children deserve?

Maddie was not brought up in a religious family, but during her time in Ethiopia, the cradle of Christianity, she had gained an affinity and a sense of connection that had opened her up to a level of spirituality. She'd embraced the aspects of the faith that resonated with her soul.

But more than anything, she prayed to the bigger power, to save Manu.

She wanted him to be free himself and escape from the demons that lived within him. She prayed for his mental health, his peace of mind and his chance to live life. To love and be loved. No matter how much her heart wanted to believe that better things would be coming for him, the reality was dark. Manu's escapism behaviour went from bad to worse. The drink, the drugs and his sexual exploits became intolerable.

He fathered a child with another woman who was employed at the same hotel where Maddie worked.

I felt sick at the thought of that and I could not bear what Maddie had gone through in her marriage. She had endured all that alone, with no one she could trust or who could understand her, or whom she could turn to.

Maddie continued her saga.

Getting sex with almost anyone was within easy reach for Manu, who was very gentle on the eye. Tall and handsome and as it was blatantly clear, well endowed. Manu could not seem to keep his rearing stallion in his stable, nor his fist in his pocket. When Maddie was working at the hotel or spending time in her art gallery, Manu would go out to play, even if he had promised to watch their daughters at home. Maddie could not rely on him anymore and took on a babysitter for when she was out. Manu was too drunk to keep his infidelity a secret. Everyone knew. And they all stared at Maddie as she went around the town. But she didn't see them. And if she did, she reminded herself it was simply her little unit that mattered and it could not sink. She had to keep her sanity and strength, though it was impossibly difficult.

Manu pushed hard to show fate that it was him who was paving the way to destruction, not a greater power. Maddie told me that Manu wanted to feel he was the one in charge of driving his personal downfall. Naturally she would have done anything if she could to stop him from disaster, but she couldn't.

Nobody could. Manu had decided. He was in charge. Of pain.

Three months after the terrible turmoil had truly kicked off, Manu went to New York for work. After his photoshoot he reportedly lost the plot after incessant rounds of Kamikazes. Having not had anything to eat, or so it seemed to the photographer, who had joined him in the bar of one of the boutique hotels that shall remain nameless, Manu first flew high and then crashed and burned. Utterly blitzed, he just about made it to his room. Manu managed to open the door and take his clothes off. He must have mistaken the soft velvet throw covering at the foot end of bed, for a blanket. He partly covered himself with it and passed out next to the bed. He was so drunk when he entered the room, that he never realised that the door of his hotel suite was left wide open behind him, before falling to the ground in a drunken stupor.

Next morning, he opened his eyes when he heard a noise in the room. Two girls were taking photographs of him. Manu was still too inebriated to be fully aware what was going on, but compos mentis enough to know he was naked with two unidentified women in his presence. His morning glory, erect and partly covered, took centre stage in what seemed like a photoshoot. Picking up on the vibe that something was not quite right, Manu tried to cover his manhood. The two girls, young fans of the beautiful Manu Model perhaps, started to stroke his naked skin as he lay on the chocolate coloured carpet of the hotel suite.

"You are a caramel prince," one of the girls whispered in his ear as she stroked his dark curls. "You work so hard. And you are so hard right now."

As she spoke the words, she slid her hand down to his private parts which, on reflection, Maddie said, had not been so private over the past treacherous months.

The girls stroked Manu as he lay on the carpeted floor. He

had not had this much care and attention for some time. The touch of a woman he had not set out to impress threw him back to when he was sixteen. That boy had responsibility and grief laden upon him. All he wanted was the hug of his mother who, in turn, was grieving the departure of her husband and the loss of her twins. Manu's blurred mind reconnected with his childhood feelings. Softly, slowly, and unexpectedly, he started to cry. Tears rolled down his handsome cheeks. The girl who was stroking his hair, started to lick the salt of sadness from his cheeks.

"It's OK," she said. "We love you."

With that she pulled back the golden coloured throw which partly concealed Manu's manhood and went down on him. All the while, the other girl was filming. When Manu was about to cum, the girl withdrew, capturing Manu's full crescendo eruption in one potent recording.

Then turning the camera on herself, she said, "There you go, Suki, you stupid cow. You didn't think we could hit a million likes on all the channels. But this should do it!"

With that she pointed the camera one more time at Manu, lying bemused and empty on the floor.

While recording, she said, "Awesome Cock, Manu! Thank you for your spectacular performance."

The girls then left the room, closing the door behind them, having released the unedited content with one tap of the posting button into cyberspace.

Never to be retrieved.

By the time Manu returned to Ethiopia, the clip was streaming across continents. Manu's career was now over. His marriage already was. For Maddie, this latest disaster was beyond the pale. It was the straw that broke the camel's back. Maddie told Manu that she and the girls were moving out. He went mad and became physically abusive. She realised this was not going to be straightforward. Now he knew of her intent to leave, he was getting anxiety attacks and started to say that he was a changed man. It was a scary time for Maddie. She did not resign from her job, as word would get out and Manu may have found out and stopped her.

Or worse.

She plotted and planned in utter silence. Maddie had to feign a family crisis and had to ask her father to directly communicate with Manu. He would have to say that Maddie was urgently needed in Germany. Only if the patriarch requested it would Manu allow Maddie to travel. She knew he would not listen to her, as she was a woman. The message from her father did the trick. Manu's tribal DNA could not refuse a request from the patriarch. Manu agreed to let Maddie go.

She eventually arrived in Germany where she settled into a small apartment which served as a landing pad to get her bearings. Through positivity and tenacity, manifestation and reconnection, Maddie managed to put herself back together. She came out of it all determined to propel herself forward in the most positive ways. She vowed never to rely on one source of income in the future. Or on a cheating, destructive man.

When she had finished speaking, I sat perfectly still.

"How utterly horrific, dearest Maddiebärchen. I am so very sorry. Will you promise that you will call me whenever you are passing through dark times? Never again, I hope, but promise me that, Maddikins. Please."

"I will, Viv." Maddie responded. "I was happy to be with

you ten years ago and I am grateful that our friendship has stood the test of time."

"It has, Maddie, but you should have called me, you nutty doughnut, you bloody Berliner."

We got up from our mattresses and hugged each other. Then we both teared up, in simple gratitude for each other. I knew and Maddie knew that we could rely on each other. Always. For anything.

"Let's go and grab our swimming costumes and hit the pool in *La Résidence.* Most of the others will be there too. It's an indoor pool, which is lucky as it's too cold to swim outside."

We closed the door on room 111. It felt symbolic.

"Goodbye to Manu and hello to you, Mads, you Mad Hatter."

"Yes, good riddance. And let's look forward to new adventures."

Steamy Steam Room

We walked to the Annex to pick up our swimsuits and set off for *Hôtel La Résidence*.

We saw that Majida and Coco were in the pool holding glasses of Champagne. No surprise there. We joined them. Coco filled some fresh glasses, which were on standby on the edge of the pool. "Reinard is getting some more bottles," she purred.

We chatted about the evening before and we enjoyed our chilling out and enjoying our time.

After a while, Maddie and I decided to go to check out the jacuzzi. *La Résidence* had certainly upgraded its facilities since we all lived on the mountain. As we came round into the Spa area which had a lovely fresh mountain scent, we caught Bash, Alex and Theo, butt naked, belting out of the sauna and bombing into the ice-cold plunge pool. It was hilarious. They were acting like teenagers. Laughing their heads off. In their boisterous joy, they were unaware that we had arrived on the scene. All three of them shouted in their loud male voices as they hit the icy cold water and scrambled to get out as soon as possible. Maddie and I stood there observing it all.

The fact that all three of them were naked felt a bit bizarre. I remembered them as boys aiming to be men thirty years ago, but now they were grown up. Very grown up I should say.

Bash noticed Maddie and me.

"Come on in, ladies," he coaxed. "We need to do this ritual a few times. A little detox of the poison from last night before we do it all again later. We used to just keep going in a 48 hour marathon session. These days we need to shock our bodies into oblivion before we can retox."

Bash divebombed one more time and then he pulled himself up on his arms and clambered out of the plunge pool.

"Enough ice cold torture," he said. "I prefer heat," he said, winking at me.

Bash was clearly totally comfortable in his own skin. He sauntered over and said hello. Theo and Alex said hi too. Without trying to hide their manhood they wrapped a towel around their hips.

"How about a session in the sauna?" Theo said to Maddie in particular. She smiled at him and followed him into the sauna. Alex and Bash went in there too.

Saunas weren't my thing.

I took the last towel to wrap myself in and sat down on the chair facing outwards, and looked through the window at the scenery beyond. The sun was reflecting on the snow making the white cover glisten. As I sat there by myself for a little while, smiling about the *Boys in the Buff* and that look Theo has just given to Maddie, my mind went off on its usual journey and I got lost in my thoughts.

I always felt there was a little frisson between those two,

Maddie and Theo. I don't know if anything ever occurred. In retrospect I believe I may have often mentioned to Maddie that Theo was just like a brother to me and I could not imagine anyone fancying him.

I saw how Maddie smiled back at Theo, when he caught her eye. Maddie had teared up earlier when she told me the sad saga of her husband Manu. But when she looked at Theo, with her deep chestnut *Liza Minnelli's*, Maddie looked bright and happy. I noted the change in her and felt a sense of happiness on her behalf. Maddie deserved all the best and had had to put up with so much.

We all have experienced heartache, challenges, and pain.

Neither Maddie nor I were an exception in that regard. But we were lucky to have embedded belief systems that allowed us to see the light in the dark and to feel safe in the knowledge that we could overcome the difficult and daunting situations that life threw at us. And to come out stronger.

While pain whether physical or of the heart, was hard to bear, I knew for sure that without deep pain and loss there were no grooves etched into your soul.

Grooves allowed the needle of life to dance and create music. There was no melody without pain. It was that simple; though not always welcome, the principle can be easily understood. After rain, there is sunshine. After dark, there is dawn. After the storm, the world feels refreshed and cleansed, and can shine again.

As far as I could see contrasts were intrinsically embedded within the laws of nature and I lived by them. Life consists of ups and downs. The tides in the sea, the emergence of spring after winter, the smile after tears. I used to think everybody knew that. But I was wrong. Not everyone is blessed to be safe in that knowledge, to take the rough with the smooth and to know in their heart of hearts that it will be all right in the end.

If it was not alright it was not the end.

After the story Maddie told me about Manu, I realised that not everyone felt that way. Maddie did, but her ex-husband did not.

Manu never knew the truth of life, the rhythm. He was simply doing time.

"Vivikaaaaaaah, *habibti*. Come on into the sauna," Bash called out.

I woke up from my musings. My little emerald-green jade man nestled between my breasts.

I didn't plan to wear him to go swimming but I figured he had survived more extreme circumstances before he was robbed from a pre-Columbian grave. I didn't want to lose him or leave him in the locker in the dressing room so I was wearing him around my neck.

"I am not really into dry heat," I teased Bash. "Wet is a better proposition. I will go for the steam room if you care to join me."

I had never felt confident around Bash during our college days. I'd been intrigued by him, attracted perhaps, yet had always been warned off him by Theo.

As if reading my mind, Bash says, "Great idea Vivika, but let's not tell Uncle Theo or he will interfere again just like he did when we were at school. I don't think Grandpa should have an opinion about us. So, let's make sure he doesn't know."

Bash walked over to me. "Excuse me for openly looking at your mountain range, they are lovely as far as I can see. The twin peaks I never got to properly feast my eyes on and your gloriousness I never got to taste, thanks to bloody Theo."

Bash grinned. I shot him a *behave yourself, don't trespass beyond acceptability* kind of look, but smiled at the same time. He winked at me, acknowledging my implied and unspoken comment.

"More importantly who is that lucky little chap tucked in between your beautiful breasts? It should not be him who is green, it should be me. I am quite jealous; I must admit. Is there any chance you will take him off at some stage over the next twenty four hours and allow me to feel what snug feels like between your magnificent bosoms?"

"Mish maqoul!" I blurted out, "You are unbelievable!"

"I know I am for sure. They all tell me that. But where did you pick up your Arabic?"

"I live between Europe and the Middle East. I have done so for years and still do."

"Good to know that my early influence on you already impacted your choices in life. Clearly, I inspired you in terms of embracing the Arab World though you never embraced me," he continued to flirt. "Let us go and get steamy in the steam room. I want to hear all about your *Arabian Carpet Ride of Life*. It will no doubt be colourful. Finally, I get to spend time with you without Theo."

"Not a bad word about Theo, Bash. He is my brother and solid as a rock."

"He is the one who gave you that little man, made of gemstone, you have around your neck, isn't he? It looks like a bit of jade trade to me but I must say I cannot think of a more kissable neck he could have graced it with."

106

"I will go into the Turkish bath with you, as long as you stop talking nonsense."

"Tammam. Mumtaez," he said, which translates as, *'OK. Great'.*

He continued, "Let's get up close and comfortable in the Hammam." He unwrapped his towel and stood naked in front of me.

While looking at me he hung up his towel on the designated hook. He opened the glass door to the steam room and looked back at me. "Are you coming? Take off that swimming costume, hang up your towel and follow me."

I had not planned on going in naked but it seemed a bit silly not to. So, I stepped out of my swimsuit, hung it up along with my towel on the hook next to Bash's and went in. I was a little bit uncomfortable as the steam was not yet thick, though after a few minutes I could only make out the contours of Bash as the evaporation blurred my vision and we settled into a conversation. Shrouded by steam and without seeing him, I felt free to talk.

I recalled being flown to the Maldives years ago. A hotel owner of two villa resorts contacted me. I was sitting in the hairdressing salon of the hotel where I used to work, when I received a call from Mr Ahmed. I didn't know him. My hair was in foils as I was having highlights put in. The man said he was the Maldivian owner of the resorts and he was looking for a person to look after sales and marketing teams in the Maldives. I told him straight up that I was not interested in being based in the middle of the Indian Ocean in the centre of nowhere. He asked me why not. I told him that as a salesperson, I should be based in the source markets. Not in the place where guests came who have already been sold to. I always found this practice bizarre.

I remembered doing a stint with a new hotel on the Dead Sea in Jordan. I was based in the Rift Valley. Looking out over the rocks, sheep, and the Dead Sea. '*Dead*' being the operative word in terms of people to sell to, at least. Where the hell would I meet any prospects there? It was against all common sense and whenever logic was defied, I typically switched off to any proposition.

I like out of the box thinking. Not stupidity.

Mr Ahmed elaborated and told me why the position would work well and was insistent that I should come over for a few days, then decide whether to join his company.

"I am saying politely to you Mr. Ahmed, that the Maldives are not for me."

"If you give me three days of your time. I will pay for your flights, accommodation, and food. Just to be able to show you what we have."

The hairdresser opened a few foils to check my hair colour and urged me to hang up, he did not want the dye to turn my hair the wrong colour. He gestured that it was time to rinse the dye off. He looked at me in the mirror pleading in a camp and exaggerated fashion. He looked like he was shampooing my hair already simulating the action with his hands behind my head.

"Mr Ahmed, I need to go but if you really want me to come over, though I have no interest in the position or location, then feel free to text me. I have three days I can give you. But now I must go. Thank you for your call."

Bizarrely that same afternoon, with my hair all done, I

received a text message.

'Please send me your email address. I will send flight details.'

I went with the flow and ended up meeting Mr Ahmed in the Maldives. He flew me to the newest resort, still under construction, but it was awesome. However, it was much too remote. In that lay the beauty for the guests of course. A total getaway and escape from the world, in the lap of luxury.

It took us two flights from Male Airport to get to the Atoll, then a forty minute speedboat ride to the hotel.

A top luxury remote resort may be nice for the inside of a week for a break, but to be stuck in paradise for any longer than that sounded like hell to me.

I have often worked remotely, meaning from a laptop wherever I might be, though not thousands of miles from any form of regular civilisation. What if I wanted to get a bar of chocolate from a supermarket? I would have to do the same journey. No way I would consider it. I had been clear with Mr Ahmed and I still felt the same. We flew back at the end of the day.

By the time the speedboat had taken us back to the closest airport, it was turning dark. We boarded the first of the two flights back to Male. I chatted easily with Mr Ahmed as we taxied towards the runway. Then the captain dimmed all the lights for take-off as was the regulation for flight departures during hours of darkness. As a result, I could not see my fellow passenger, Mr Ahmed. Just like in the steam room, the visual element of the conversation was no longer there. It allowed you to speak even more freely, I felt. I told the CEO that I was happy to work with him as a consultant, though not in the Maldives. He asked me why I would not want to take on a permanent role.

I explained that apart from the location, I do not like the hierarchy and politics of being employed. I told him that I enjoyed big brains, strategic minds, and intelligent conversation. Like we were having.

I said to Mr. Ahmed, "Just as we are sitting here, I feel comfortable talking to you about anything I like without having to change my words for political reasons. This is how I want to be, how I am at my best. When airs and graces are disregarded and we can get on with the business in hand."

Our chat in the dark was revealing to me. I realised that I like men who are in charge, who are driven and have a good brain. I remembered my times with Captain James and General Salim. Not that Mr Ahmed, with respect, was in their category, but he was a determined man and open to dialogue and exchanging thoughts. Even in the dark.

Now, here on the mountain, in the steam room with Bash, I wondered whether I would get to know Bash better as we are both shrouded from view. Would I find out more about this guy I had a soft spot for, but never really got to know?

"So, Vivika *habibti,* we finally get to be in one place together. The lovely untouchable Vivika and me, the scoundrel Arab boy. Who would have thought? Have you been with an Arab man before, Vivi?"

The steam was now so thick, I could not see Bash. I didn't say anything as I remembered General Salim. The Omani who stirred me beyond words. Or used to.

"It seems that my chance to be your first Arab conquest has passed. Am I right?"

I didn't speak.

"Who is this Arab man who stole your heart? I can hear from

your silence that he ran deep."

"It's a long story. A cherished and a sensitive one. Discretion is required. As you know. The wrong idea and a loose lip can cause serious damage in the Arab world. I don't want to say anything about him nor am I at liberty to do so."

"Wisely spoken Vivi. You have my respect. Not many Vikings know that."

"I am not a Viking. You need to go a bit more south."

"That sounds like a great idea. If your body is a map and the mountain range where your little man enjoys his days is north, then let me find out for myself where *slightly south* on your map would be."

My cheeks were flushed as puss purred.

Bash couldn't see me and I couldn't see him. But a steam room was the appropriate place to be. I felt him move towards me, boldly, with confidence. I could feel his naked body as he sidled up to me. He felt my face with his fingers and touched my lips. Then he kissed me and started exploring.

"Allow me to check the weather in the southern regions. I hear it is wet, this time of year."

"I think you will find it to be tropical. Wet and hot."

"That is my kind of climate," Bash whispered.

He kissed me on my lips, cupped my breast and moved down beyond my belly button. He sat on his knees in front of me and placed my legs over his shoulders. He went down on me. I could not see him and he could not see me. But his presence was powerful as he took his time to pleasure me. I was lost in the moment as he took me higher and higher. I vaguely regained my sense of where I was when I heard someone outside the door.

Not now. Please God. Not now.

Even with the sound outside Bash stayed where he was, taking me to the edge. And over. I gasped in ecstasy as the door to the steam room was pushed open.

Thank God it wasn't a second earlier.

Flirtus Interruptus

The door was left open and the steam instantly reduced in intensity.

"Here you are, you two," Theo said. "I thought I told you to leave my sister alone all those years ago. I did not think I had to repeat myself."

"Jeez, Theo, now who is the Arab, protecting his sister? She is a grown woman and I think perhaps it is time to let the lady make her own decisions? Or did you have plans with Vivi all those years ago and she rejected you? You clearly tried to impress her by giving her that little magic man that lives between her breasts."

"Stay away from Vivika. I love you like a brother but don't be the conman with her. She cannot be involved."

"As if you are clean as the driven snow," Bash replied. "Look who is calling the kettle black."

"In family some things are sacred. And you are crossing the line."

"Sacred, indeed. Like that jade antiquity relic, you gave her. Or are you simply trying to smuggle that too and to see whether she could be your blue-eyed girl to open new routes by sending her on a test-run? To see if you can trust her?"

"Enough!" Theo shouted.

I had no idea what the hell was going on. The steam was fast fading. The room lacked oxygen.

"Guys let's get out of here. I need some air."

"I would love to give you some *air, habibti.*"

It was quite likely, I realised, that Theo would not know that '*air*' in colloquial Arabic means, '*dick*'.

As I left the steam room Theo and Bash did not follow me. I heard their raised voices. The door was still open.

Theo shouted at Bash, "When we started all those years ago, we named our own 'untouchables'. Mine are my family, Vivi, and Maddie, as you well know Bash! This has not changed. I expect you to respect our agreement." His voice became fainter as I heard him say, "Your untouchables are your mother and Anna. You did not look after them and lost them both. For that, I am sorry. But it does not mean that because you have no one, that you can touch my inner circle."

The door then closed and sealed itself.

Whatever else was being said remained between the two men.

I shivered as I took my towel from the hook and wrapped myself in it.

"What's up, Viv?" Maddie asked, as she appeared, returning from the locker room, already dressed. "Did you get steamy with Bash in there?"

"Steamy is the understatement of the century."

I locked arms with Maddie.

"Let's get out of here and go up the mountain for some sunshine. It feels a bit oppressive in this place." Before Maddie could respond, I said, "Don't ask Maddiebärchen, let's just go. I could do with just you and me and the view from above the clouds. I know there are plenty of people to play with. At the last count there were 273 registered attendees from all the years. But frankly all I want is to be with you with a glass of white in my hand. And the sun on my face. I could really do with your take on this Mads, I am officially confused."

"Sure thing, Bussi. Seems like something happened. Don't worry about it. I am sure that whatever occurred is just a wobble. These boys may think they are men but when they disagree on a point or take issue, the best thing is to leave them to it. Whatever it is, it will blow over. Theo and Bash have always been good friends with great similarities uniting them and at the same time, with great differences dividing them. Theo is fiercely loyal to you and very protective. Consider yourself privileged. He is awesome."

"When we get to the top of the mountain dear Maddie, I hope you will confide in me about what is cooking between you and Theo."

Maddie blushed. "OK, Buss. I am not sure, though it would be great to have a think out loud with you. Hope we can find some deckchairs in the sunshine and take our space before dinner and disco tonight."

Mountain Air

We took the chairlift rather than the télécabine to go up the mountain. It would not take us all the way to the very top, but we knew the lower level restaurant was smaller and nestled in the basin out of the wind. If there was any sun, which there was, *La Neige* was the best place to do some proper winter-sport tanning. In addition, we got to chat together, see no one else, and feel the sun and the breeze as we were transported up the mountain.

Having come straight from *La Résidence*, we were not wearing our skis. We asked the operator to stop the lift as we got to the top. Normally as you arrived, you pointed your skis upwards, lifted the safety bar and got up as you reached the precipice at the end of the lift, and then you could ski down to the restaurant. On this day, we traipsed through the snow that was fast turning to sludge. As the restaurant was facing south, the snow deteriorated quickly in the afternoon sun. For avid skiers therefore this slope was not of interest on a day like that day. But for us, it was perfection.

Quiet, warm, and sunny, it was quite stunningly beautiful.

We settled into a bottle of excellent, local, dry white wine, which was *pétillant,* slightly sparkling, and we enjoyed a plate of *fromage et charcuterie,* cheese and slices of air dried meat and pickles. A very Swiss tapa style snack. Maddie admitted that she had always held a torch for Theo and that she had even been in an undercover relationship with him during the last term of school.

I was flummoxed.

"You what?"

"Yup. I did. I should have said at the time, but really what was the point? It was the end of the year. Our short lived liaison would not go anywhere. And you always said you did not understand girls who fancied Theo. And I thought, why come clean? So, we did what we did and then we lost touch. Of course, I wondered whether I would feel the same about him if I ever were to see him again. You would not believe the flip my tummy did when you told me your Costa Rican Dutch brother had confirmed. And I admit he still has that certain *'je ne sais quoi'.*"

"You dark horse, you! It certainly seems like there are some sparks flying now. You only have a few days on the mountain with him. Does that matter?"

"No, not at all. I don't want to commit to anything. I have not been with anyone since I met Manu, so that is going back some twenty years now. Since I moved to Germany last September half a year ago now, I have been taking my time to process what happened or at least partly. It has been one hell of a roller coaster. And of course I have Eshe and Emmanuelle to think about. Although as I am talking to you, I realise now that they are pretty much the age we were when we first landed on this Mountain. My God, Bussi! Think about that. I hope they will make better choices than I did."

"Do you regret the choices you made?"

Maddie took a sip of her wine as she thought about my question.

"You know what, Buss? I would not change anything. I felt life, I gave birth, I loved, I travelled. I have my girls and my friends and family, and you. What is there not to be grateful for? How about you Buss - do you have any regrets?"

"Maybe that I never got together with Bash," I joked. "But there is still time. You better take care of Theo so that the path is clear for my little romp with that blond Arab. Not that I have not been warned. I fell for an Arab man and it almost killed me. But there is something about them that appeals to me."

I took a sip of my wine and continued. "By the way Mads, Theo said something to Bash about you and me. He said he'd told Bash all those years ago that his own untouchables were his family and the two of us."

"Good God!" Maddie said. "I wonder what that was all about? Sounds mafia-like. I know that we never thought either of these two blond boys were angels, but this is intriguing. We may need to tread a little carefully and probe. In more ways than one. Remember how we learnt to do that. Ask, then shut up and listen. Always a challenge for us Bussi, but perhaps one of the most valuable lessons we learnt on this mountain."

"I know from experience I can be gullible and naïve. Do you remember that day when we went to *Le Pâtisserie* and that guy Mike who I quite fancied from college had powder sugar above his lip and on his nose? I asked him, *'Mike what sweet cake have you bitten into? You are covered in powder sugar.'* He stopped playing Backgammon and ran off to the bathroom. I remember thinking that his reaction was a bit over the top. Only later did I come to understand that the boys at the college were always sniffing cocaine and that white stuff was nothing to do with any type of *gâteau*."

"Oh yes I remember it well. Mike was playing Backgammon with Lisa. Though we liked her we hated the fact that she always became interested in the same men that any of us liked. That was the case with Mike. I remember Lisa asking who he was. I don't think she even really knew Mike, but she made it her business. She was and is very good looking, though that was not an attractive characteristic. Do you remember that we simply started to pretend that we liked random people to her and she would then pursue them? In the end the joke was on us. I guess she was insecure. Thank goodness she's grown out of it. I think she is a decent sort now. Married and settled. She writes."

"You are the sharp one with the suspicious mind, Maddie. I think we need to see what is going on. Let us say nothing to Bash, or even to Theo, much as it feels wrong to be investigating his motives a bit deeper."

"The number of times that Bash specifically mentioned my jade amulet was a bit suspect I thought. Bash was vague about almost everything else, except for what he would like to do to me. I have to say I am not averse to the thought of a little more of the same. He's yummy. Clearly you and Theo are getting on well. Seems you picked up where you left off even though your last amorous encounter was three decades ago."

"Not entirely Buss. I never told you what happened afterwards. A few years later when I was living in Belgium before I settled into my role in Ethiopia, Theo came to Holland. A case had been raised against his elderly dad and he was sent over from Costa Rica to sort the matter out. It sounded like what you may describe as a *white collar case*. Anyhow Theo and I spent a week together. Naturally he was concerned for his father, but we still managed to have a really good time together."

When I met up with Theo after he'd been to see the family lawyer, it appeared that his dad was in big trouble. He juggled houses, art and antiquities, and other assets along those lines. In the end Theo's father was convicted, though not extradited as he was too ill to travel. He eventually died, leaving Theo to deal with matters. I asked him earlier whether he was OK and I reminded him of our time in Holland. He told me that he loved seeing me there, however, he added that he would like to leave his father's matters in the past and not talk about them. It seems he is carrying a burden. Maybe that's what is making him so jumpy around Bash?"

We talked some more about the people we had not seen for ages and the new people we had met from the years both before and after ours.

"Do you know I never knew that Coco goes by the name of Colette?" I asked.

"Really? Why?"

"Because that is her actual name, ditsy doughnut! Are you having a *Berliner Moment*? We just never knew that her full name was '*Colette Anna-Maria*'. Imagine! I knew her from the age of ten or so. We went to school together; I had no clue. I remember having lunch at her house one day after school. Her mother was an amazing cook. I can't remember what we had for main course though the dessert was fresh pineapple drizzled with kirsch. Rather a strong liquor for my pre-teenage palette, yet I found it exciting and ate my whole serving. We are talking some forty years ago now Buss. Do you realise? Fresh pineapple was not something they sold in the shops. Only canned pineapple in sweet sticky artificially produced syrup. Coco's father worked for a large oil company and had been to Central America and brought one back from his travels. He said he'd cut it down himself with a machete when he visited a plantation in Nicaragua. Her dad was in Latin America for oil business and there he was invited by a wealthy investor to spend time at the mogul's where he grew acres of pineapples. On her father's return I was fortunate enough to sample that gorgeous fruit. From then on, I became interested to see what Latin America was like. We knew about Suriname and the ABC islands, Aruba, Bonaire and Curaçao, off the coast of Venezuela, due to the fact there was a link to Dutch history. Coco's father managed to make that part of the world come to life for me. I always loved going to Coco's house. Her mother was from Singapore, she was beautiful and refined. I always felt I was in a super welcoming and exotic household when I was at Coco's home.

Some years after we graduated Coco and I decided to go skiing on our collective favourite mountain. We booked our rooms at *La Résidence* before the grand refurb. We set off from Holland and continued through Germany. When we arrived at the Swiss border, we had to buy a *vignette*; the equivalent of a toll sticker, allowing us to use the Swiss motorways. As we slowed down and got to the booth to buy the sticker, for some unknown reason, Coco looked in the rear mirror of the car. She let out what I can only describe as a yelp. She leaned her head out of the driver seat window, shouting "Patrick!" Then, she stopped the car with a jolt, jumped out and the guy in question ran towards her. They hugged. I saw him gesturing her to get back in the car, doing an impression of drinking a coffee while pointing at a roadside."

I took a sip of my wine and continued my story, "Coco told me it was her brother Patrick. He was moving house from London to Geneva. She had no idea until she happened to look at the road behind her and saw him, in that very second, crossing the road. It was bizarre, yet not entirely mind blowing. We live our lives and surprises, coincidences, signs, and symbols, seem to manifest themselves at various times in different places. I personally find it comforting. And magical. I believe in energy and being connected in ways we never thought possible. I don't try to rationalise it; I just enjoy it. Miracles are marvellous and magnificent. Yet normal."

Maddie smiled.

I smiled back at her and said, "I will have to get used to Coco being called something else. Talking of names, do you know that Bash is not Bash's first name or in fact his surname?"

"What do you mean?" We have always called him Bash."

"You'd be surprised to see what I came across doing the registration. Bash is short for *Bashir,* his surname. His first name - wait for it - is *Amin,* meaning trustworthy or honest."

"Bash - trustworthy? We may like him and enjoy his company but suggesting that he is a saint with the truth may be a little farfetched. Then again, I think Theo too has some untold stories. Tell me Viv, do you think Theo has any deep secrets?"

"Apart from the many children he must have fathered over the years. I would not suggest he is clean as a whistle but I think it safe to play your tune on his," I joked.

"You cheeky moo! I'll have you know I am quite the flautist when I find the instrument that resonates."

"I am quite sure of that Mad Maddie. I happen to think you and Theo are well suited. Make music and magic while on our mountain, I say."

"Funny to think we would have had similar friendships, crushes, and crises, had we been in any other class and had not graduated in the class of 1986. The other year's students are close to each other, just like we are. Weird to think we probably would not be friends, had we not come to the Marvellous Mountain at the same time. In addition, it was our luck to be neighbours which makes our friendship even more special."

"When I count my blessings..." I started and waited for Maddie to finish.

"I count you twice," she said.

I had a card on my desk in my room on which my mother had written me a message for when I first arrived at the hotel school. My mother always tucked a precious message into my luggage whenever I travelled. It meant the world to me. And this card had touched my heart. Maddie loved it too when she first read it. Even after all these years, she seamlessly completed the words of our little shared saying.

"Love you Mads, I am eternally happy we reconnected. I guess we should pack up. Now the sun has dipped behind the mountain, I am freezing. Let's go down and make it back to school. We need a warmup and a bath before we go out again. It was wonderful up here this afternoon."

"Loved it too. Perfect spot. Great catch up. Now let's land Theo and Bash for some letting our hair down. Hope they have settled their differences and all is well again."

Room 111

We arrived back at school where the bar was heaving just like the night before.

Bash walked straight over to me, "Hi *habiti*. You are just the person I want to spend my time with. Let us use the opportunity to escape from Theo's prying eyes. We have at least an hour or so before dinner."

"Why is Theo so hell bent on you and me not hanging out?"

"Hanging out I don't think would be an issue," Bash said. "Theo has a soft spot for you. He would never have given you that Mayan Man if he didn't. It is a rare little statue. You don't just give that to anyone. It means something more. For sure. Unless Dutch people share treasures without wanting a return on investment. From my side, I question that. Maybe it is my Syrian or Iraqi background but I don't trust that there is nothing there. Why else would he have interrupted us like that in the steam room today, when I was tasting your gorgeousness? He interrupted our flirtations and delicious interaction. What do you say, Viv? I still have the key to my old room."

"You still have your dorm key thirty years later?" I was amazed. "Why would you keep it?"

"I had some of my happiest times here on the mountain. Away from Iraq and away from Syria. There was a load of hard reality going down at the time. My family shipped me off to Switzerland. I insisted on having my cars and my toys. And that was it. I ended up here. But it was the only time in my life that I felt connected and valued for who I am. There are not that many blue eyed, fair skinned Arab boys around and I was always being used to deliver goods and packages for my father. They never stopped me at the border and I earned some money doing that. Not having to keep travelling was nice. People at school were good. We were all in the same boat and I did not stick out like a sore thumb, like I did back home. Though I never wanted to be living on some mountain in the middle of nowhere I must admit, they were the happiest years of my life."

"Wow, Bash! That was probably the most you have ever said to me in one go. I am happy you look back on our time here with warmth, but thirty years have passed. Have you not known happiness during that time?"

"Happiness is a big word. I never really feel fully happy. Somehow, I have a shell over my soul like a harness. I know people will have some psychological analysis they will let loose on me but I don't think about it too much. It is what it is. As to your question about keeping my room key, I guess it is symbolic. I want to keep those memories safe. I don't want them to be touched or taken from me. I know it is quite normal for people to take advantage of others, but I will not let them take what means this much to me."

"What do you mean, that it's normal to take advantage of others? I am allergic to opportunists. I didn't think you would be one, Bash. Maybe Theo is right? I should be careful around you."

"*Habibti* Vivika, relax. All is good. We will take a bottle of red up to room 111 and see if we have anything in common. If so, let's explore. If not, let's go back to ground zero, and have dinner and dance. No strings attached."

It was such a random situation and I must say I continued to be intrigued by Bash. With bottle and two glasses, we trundled up to Bash's old room.

"Allow me," I said, when we stopped outside room 111.

Bash looked bemused when I took out my copy of the same key from my pocket. When Maddie and I had our chat that afternoon we had also used room 111 to be away from everyone. I had wanted to return it but had not yet done so. I was pleased I had the key to room 111 still on me.

I looked at Bash, and said, "Each room always has two keys and one spare. It seems that when you took yours Bash, or stole it I should say, the people at school likely thought that two keys would still be enough and that there was no need to change the lock and go to that expense. I borrowed this key from the organising committee office and it is due to be returned tonight. But here we go, I have it on me."

I slid the key into the lock and opened the door. Bash still looked a bit taken aback.

"Seems we both have the key for room 111. Is that a sign?" Bash asked.

"Who knows? One thing I do know is that you took it without permission and I didn't."

"*Khallas,* enough philosophising Viv. Let's go in, pour some of this wine and catch up."

Bash opened the bottle of red wine and poured it in to the oversized glasses he had brought up. We raised our glasses and looked at each other.

"To more gorgeousness," Bash toasted, giving me a cheeky smile.

"To getting to know you better," I replied.

After some easy chatting, Bash asked me about the jade man. I told him Theo had given him to me all those years ago and painted the scene for Bash.

"When Theo gave the little jade man to me, he asked me to close my eyes and open the palm of my hand, which I did. When he put the item into my hand and closed my fingers around it, he asked me to keep my eyes shut. He then asked, *'What do you feel?'* "

"What did you feel?" Bash asked.

"I felt an energy softly throbbing in my hand. Like there was a pulse to whatever I was holding."

Bash looked intrigued.

"Theo said it had been stolen. He then told me that because it was given to me with good intent, all would be OK. He said the little man would protect me. He couldn't watch over me himself, so this was to be my talisman, from Theo to me."

"He was always a smooth operator, that Dutch Tico. But I must give it to him, that was nice. Are you wearing him tonight?"

"I am," I replied.

"May I see him *habibti,* that little man of yours? "

I agreed and tried to pull the leather lace over the top of my blouse but it got stuck.

"Allow me," Bash said, as he stood in front of me and started to unbutton my blouse until my breasts were partly uncovered. I held my breath and noticed my heartbeat quickening.

The little Mayan man remained snug between my boobs. Bash gently released the figurine and looked at him, while keeping the back of his warm hand against the skin between my breasts. I shivered.

"He is warm," Bash said. "And perfect as are you. I can't believe I listened to Theo. When I think that I could have had you all those years ago, I feel deprived and seriously annoyed. On the other hand, I am happy to be here with you now."

I couldn't speak.

Bash leaned into me and kissed me. It was a soft and lingering kiss. I responded.

"Now, how much do you know about Arab men?" he whispered.

"Rather more than you know," I said.

"Is that a good or a bad thing?"

"Neither, really. But I am just more aware of your charming ways. I find you Arabs attractive as a species in general, I must admit."

"Hmm. Interesting to talk about us in a generic way. I would like a glass of that red now and to relax on those mattresses under the heaters on the big balcony. I would like you to get to know *this* particular Arab much better," Bash said.

We settled on the mattress in the corner leaning against the brick of the building where we had spent such amazing times. The stone still held some of the heat from the afternoon sun, making the wall feel warm and firm against my back.

"You said you felt an energy from the little Mayan man. What did you mean by that?"

"Well, people often say that rocks and stones are dead. I think they are wrong. I believe energy pulsates all around us. In fact, I know it to be true. In the past, I had a bracelet made from turquoise stone beads that erupted in my car. Without me even touching it. The energy jolted the beads outwards as the bracelet exploded. It was a sign. Funnily enough it was related to an Arab guy whom I lost my heart to. On other occasions too, I have felt energy from stones. I was in Jordan once. For the past twenty years I have lived on and off in the Middle East and combined Europe with the Orient. I made some good friends in Jordan over that time and used to visit their friends in the Rift Valley, just south of the Dead Sea. You probably know that it is the lowest point on earth. We stopped there one day to buy the best tomatoes which we intended to dry using salt from the Dead Sea. We had fun thinking about how we were going to do that, when my friend Yousef who was from Jordan asked me whether I was interested in archaeology."

Bash's eyes lit up. "Are you interested in archaeology?" he asked.

I never would have expected this to be one of Bash's interests. He was into fast cars and guns, so it was a surprise to me.

"I love antiques and relics," he said. "Would kill for them. I will want to explore you later, but I am super keen to hear about your Jordan experiences. I want to hear your story about antiquities, relics, and hidden gems. After that I want to totally, indulgently and without more frustrations or distractions, feast on you and be captivated by your hidden cave of forbidden treasures."

"Jordan is an archaeological paradise," I laughed, trying not to focus on Bash's bold flirtations.

"Tell me more," Bash said. His words threw me back to our sales class.

I continued, "After we bought our tomatoes, we made our way to *The Dig House*. A Greek-Cypriot archaeologist, Vassilis, lived in this unlikely place. A mosaic rescued from a local site was being restored in the living room. It was a bit Bohemian. The cushions on the sofa were half on the floor, the shaggy carpet looked like a live sheep or two had just collapsed on their hooves and taken up residency. The ashtrays were full of cigarette ends. Vassilis was not home when we arrived but Yousef found the key in the usual place. Vassilis kept it in the Hebron blue glass flowerpot next to the cactus. It was placed on the window ledge round the back of the house outside the kitchen. It seemed plenty of people came and went. Archaeologist friends, Yousef, and his cronies, Vassilis's girlfriend and a few of the locals. There were all sorts of antiquities lying around the place. Yousef pointed out Islamic glass, pre-pottery wheel ceramics and various other things."

Bash listened with great interest as he filled my glass. "Interesting. Where do you say the place was?"

"Near Lot's cave, mentioned in the bible. In a place called Safi, just south of the Dead Sea."

"Would love to go there, someday. Maybe we could go together and you could be my guide."

"Who knows," I laughed and continued, "When we were about to leave Vassilis and his girlfriend rocked up and insisted we stay for a late lunch. Their car boot was full of wine and food. Another one of their friends arrived too, a guy from London who worked for the British Museum and a friend of Vassilis's. It was a hot day in the valley. The British Museum guy, George, spotted the little jade man around my neck and asked me if he could take a closer look at it. I pulled him off over my head and passed the Mayan Man to George.

'Where did you get him?' he asked. I did not say much, just as Theo had requested."

Then I recalled what Theo had told me when he'd given me the little man all those years ago and I felt a knot in my stomach. I should not be telling Bash anything about him. Then again, Theo and Bash had already discussed the topic in the steam room earlier.

I continued, "George told me that the piece was an exquisite example from the Pre-Colombian era and I should bring it to their expert at the British Museum when I was next in London. As I lived between the Middle East, London, and Amsterdam, that was easy enough for me to arrange and I agreed I would do so. We settled down into some great conversation with our glasses of wine. Vassilis and his girlfriend fixed dinner and we ended up staying overnight. Vassilis asked me if I minded sleeping in a room with ancient tomb stones. I didn't. Why would I? It turned out that the tombstones dated from the days that Jews, Greeks and Christians lived in harmony in the Great Rift Valley which runs from Ethiopia to Turkey, but you probably knew that as it passes through Lebanon too."

"Yes, I know. So, you slept in the room with a few of these tombstones?"

"There were more than a few, Bash. In fact, I remember asking Vassilis how many tombstones I would be surrounded by. He told me that there were two hundred and eighty or thereabouts. I asked him why he had all the stones at *The Dig House*. He explained he wanted to keep them safe from smugglers. Grave robbers were a significant problem in Jordan. The thieves sold the stolen relics to illegal traders, who in turn sold the antiquities at exorbitant prices. Vassilis showed me a catalogue of a gravestone just like the ones in my bedroom. One of them had been made into a coffee table and sold at auction for the equivalent of sixty thousand dollars. Now the rock that commemorated a dead person in one continent, was used to put coffee on and perhaps lines of cocaine, in a swanky New York apartment.

Vassilis was trying everything he could to keep all of Jordan's historical artifacts and antiquities in the country and he was trying to secure funds to build a museum on the Dead Sea so people could enjoy the beautiful items in Jordan, the cradle of civilisation and the rightful home of the relics and treasures. As a result, Vassilis was trying to slow down the illegal trade."

I checked in with Bash, "Am I boring you?"

"Categorically not. On the contrary, *ya habibti. Kaemli laousamahti,* keep going darling."

He topped up our glasses. "Don't forget to sip on your wine. I want to hear your stories and find you relaxed when we move into other areas of good energy later."

"Talking about energy," I say, "with all those gravestones in my room, I remember putting my hands on the jute bags in which they were kept. They're not like the modern tombstones, you know?"

"I know," Bash replied. "They're smaller, thicker, rounder, like the rocks in the Flintstones."

"Exactly! I have never met anyone who knows what they look like. How do you know?"

"Must be an Arab thing, I guess. We should know about our history and our cultural past."

"Anyway, when I put my hands on the stones, I felt a soft pulsation just like with my little Mayan man. Since that experience, I have placed my hands on any antiquity that I see. Mosaics, frescoes, jade, tombstones, beads, and glass. They all come alive when you close your eyes and feel them."

"I would come alive if you felt me too," Bash said, his voice now lower and thicker. He came towards me and took the glass of red wine out of my hand. "Close your eyes and let's see if you can pick up on the energy of my rock."

"Bash!" I exclaimed. "Don't be so crass."

"Just joking," he laughed, as he took me in his arms and kissed me. "You are lovely Vivi. I don't want to go fast with you. I reckon there are many things to explore together. For one, your love of antiquities resonates with me. Who knows, we may be able to support your friend Vassilis to erect his museum. A noble man, Vassilis. He should be helped in his quest."

"That would be something," I agreed. "A lovely thought, Bash."

"No problem dear Vivi. Now, where were we?" He kissed me again, until a loud knock on the door stopped us in our tracks.

Tribute

"**B**ash! Open. Hurry!" we heard Alex say. "Dinner has started and Theo noticed that you and Vivi are missing. Get your ass down to the canteen. Come in separately. He is out for your blood. He said he warned you."

Bash shouted back, "Give me a minute."

He turned back to me, kissed me again and said, "Theo may not like this. But I like you. Let us not say a word and we will figure out our next steps. Go ahead of me. I will see you later."

I left room 111 and passed by the bathroom. I was about to go inside to fix my lipstick, when I saw Maddie walking towards me in the corridor, looking for me.

"Where have you been?" she asked.

"A bit of a story. Cover for me. I can't bear the idea of drama again. The steam room saga at lunchtime was more than enough."

"No worries. We will say that you were asked to deliver some words tonight and that you were writing and trying to practice your after dinner speech."

"What are you talking about Maddie. I haven't been asked to do that and even if I were, I wouldn't have the foggiest idea of what to say."

"Listen I remember you did a brilliant speech on the Scandinavian night, thirty years ago. I know you wrote it, practiced it, and recorded it at the time because you made me listen to you rehearsing it. I remember too, that you took a few shots of Aquavit, that killer Scandinavian paint stripper excuse of a drink, to limber up before you were on. Why don't you just take a shot or two and do the same thing. That way Theo will never suspect that you were with Bash. Because that is who you were with, right?"

"Right. Bloody hell, this is not good. I just wanted to have dinner and some fun."

"I am having fun at the thought of you standing on one of the canteen chairs so many years later. Only a few of us will recall that speech, as the other years weren't there. I will tell Theo and take it from there. Maybe he'll forget and your bacon will be saved. Now hurry, get into the canteen. I reserved you a spot next to Coco. And pretend to the rest of them too, that you were asked to address the crowd. You need to live the scenario Viv. Believe it is true and they will believe you. As you said. Enough drama."

I made my way into the canteen, having grabbed a piece of paper out of the pigeonhole where the post had been sorted. The A4 piece of paper was the right size. I also grabbed a pen and pretended to be reading the paper as I walked into the canteen. I felt Theo's eyes on me but I ignored him and settled down next to Coco. I demonstratively folded the paper and tucked it inside my bra.

The first course arrived. Bash has not yet come down. Only when the main course was served did he make an appearance, wearing different clothes and smoking a cigar. He seemed perfectly relaxed and settled down next to Alex and Theo. He offered them a Cohiba each. Soon everything appeared to have settled and was back to normal. The boys cut and lit their cigars. Smoking cigars halfway through dinner was hardly well mannered but anything seemed to go here, even with those who were supposed to have been taught some basic etiquette.

After the main course and before dessert, Malcolm who was the DJ in the school disco thirty years ago, stood up and tapped the back of his spoon against his wine glass.

"Speech!" some people shouted. Then, others joined in and the word started to become a mantra. Malcolm raised his hands and ushered the crowd into silence.

"Thank you dear Reunionists for coming back to The Mountain. We are almost coming out of the other side of our wonderful long weekend. It was great to see you still swinging your hips to the Golden Oldies and I expect you to boogie your little socks off until dawn on our last night together. Brunch will be served from the crack of dawn, as long as Dawn doesn't mind."

Everybody laughed and cheered. Malcom's joke about Dawn's crack was totally in line with the mood of the night. Relaxed, silly, fun, and encouraging everyone to let their hair down.

"After that *The Reunion* will officially be finished," Malcolm says.

"Boo!" we all shouted, while laughing.

Malcolm calmed the crowd to order and said, "Finished

- until we meet up again, next time. I hope in the not too distant future."

This was met by cheers and raised glasses.

Once again, Malcolm, in his amiable way, commanded quiet and continued, "Before we serve dessert, we have a tribute from one of our graduates, from the Class of 1986."

"Yay!" the canteen erupted again.

My heart sank. I knew I was up next. What the hell was I going to say?

"I would like to welcome to the front, Ms Vivika. Come on over Vivi."

"Vivi, Vivi," the crowd begin to chant my name over and over.

There was nothing else for it.

I looked at Maddie pleadingly. She gave me a 'Sorry darling, but what can I do' smile. I took a large gulp of my wine. Maddie positioned a Schnapps in front of me, which I downed in one. I stood up. Malcolm gestured me to come over to him as he placed a wooden dining chair in front of the buffet, to offer me a view over the lines of tables that stretched from the entrance to the exit. It was a full house. Malcolm helped me up onto the chair and passed me the microphone. I began.

"I have been asked to make a tribute to the men."

A huge cheer erupted. The males in the room vocally expressed their appreciation. When they calmed down, it was time to bluff my way out of an undoubtedly rubbish situation.

On the hoof, I improvised, "Thirty years ago you were still boys, you revered us girls but we saw you as toys. Still pimple rich and wrinkle free, you wished for us your willies to free. You thought you were big but you were still small, but now we admit we see you stand tall. You developed into men of pride and repute. And are now rather hunkier, there is no dispute. We are blessed and delighted to be on the top of this rock. No, I won't now be obvious and rhyme that with cock. We are here to enjoy old friends as well as the new and remember old times and our marvellous view. On top of the world and blessed from above, may we forever share our memories of our *Mountain of Love*."

I raised my glass and everyone cheered.

Glasses were topped up and Malcolm played, "*It's Raining Men*" by The Weather Girls, on full volume.

He turned the music down temporarily like a professional DJ and said, "Thank you Ms. Vivi, for your tribute. Let's take it away."

Malcolm pumped up the music again. Alex helped me down from my speech podium and I went back to where the girls were sitting. People spontaneously got up and started dancing.

Johnny stole the show, giving it all he's had while shouting, "Viva La Domenica!"

"Take it away, Johnny!" Malcolm belted out from the mic and the floor went loose.

The attention was no longer on me. Thank goodness.

"Bloody hell, girl!" Maddie says. "How the hell did you pull that act off? It has nothing to do with your Scandi speech way back when. But you did it! I am impressed!"

Majida and Coco high-fived me and I heaved a sigh of relief. I didn't think anyone else noticed. Theo caught my eye and winked at me, giving me an approving nod of his head and a double thumbs up.

Thank God, I think Theo bought it.

I turned and saw Bash looking at me. He seemed to have a whole new level of interest in me. He was yummy, but really – I didn't need this tension. What would it lead to, anyway? Was a bit of fun with Bash worth sacrificing my long standing friendship with Theo for?

I didn't think so.

As the evening developed, we all had too much to drink. Theo and Maddie were going crazy on the dance floor.

Though Theo was Dutch, he had lived out in Costa Rica for years. His father moved the family there when he had a dream that the Russians were going to invade Holland. Based on that dream Theo's father moved his whole family away from their Dutch home. Theo was taken out of school midway through the year and put into Spanish education where he stood out like a sore thumb with his bright blond hair, not knowing a word of the language.

The family had major investments in the Netherlands. Nonetheless, Theo's father uprooted his family and took them lock stock and barrel to Central America. Theo was ten years old at the time. He was the oldest one in our group. Maybe that's why I accepted his protective stance from the start.

Maddie was a nut on the dance floor. She had rhythm and style. She had formally learnt to ballroom dance as part of her education. But this is no Waltz, or Foxtrot. Maddie could take anything and make it her own, as she did with the new blend of Salsa and Cha-cha-cha. Theo and Maddie commanded the floor as the other Reunionists formed a circle around them, watching as the couple performed their moves. Theo kept up with Maddie brilliantly which was not an easy feat. Even though Maddie was in charge, it looked as if Theo was leading.

Such style she had, our Maddie. I could see she was laughing and, truly, she deserved happiness. She had gone through hell and now she was having a great time.

It was blissful to see.

Having given it their all, Theo and Maddie left the dance floor, holding hands. Theo sat down and pulled Maddie onto his lap. Alex had lined up a fresh beer for Theo, who took the metal beer bottle lid off with his teeth. He then spat it out on the floor and grinned at Maddie.

"You animal!" Maddie said, laughing.

Theo offered Maddie the bottle and she took a swig. She handed the beer back to him. Theo automatically placed the bottle in the usual position, against his chest almost under his right armpit. His signature stance. I watched them chatting happily and after a while Theo put the bottle down and Maddie slipped off his lap. They held hands as they left the disco dinner. By the time they had reached the door, Theo had put his arm around her shoulder and she had placed hers around his middle. They walked into the brightly lit corridor, as their silhouettes disappeared. They would not be seen again until breakfast the next day.

As if on cue, Bash joined me.

"*Habibti,* the obsessive guard has left. Let's go and finish off what we started. Room 111 revisited. What do you think?"

"I think maybe not," I replied. "Some things are clearly not meant to be."

"Vivi, I understand today was a non-starter and I don't want to talk you into anything you don't want to do. But truly, I want to see you again. Whether in Jordan or Marbella, London, or Switzerland. I was serious when I spoke to you about the museum idea. If you would like, maybe we can connect with Vassilis online and we can see what can be done. You know my family is not short of a penny or two and I have realised that I want to do more than just spend money on fun. I want to do something worthwhile, that leaves a legacy. Now is the time to make a mark. The way you talked about energy really resonates with me. Tell you what. If I behave, will you do me the honour of having a nightcap with me? We can go back to the bar. It's much quieter now. If you are more comfortable there, let's do that?"

It seemed a reasonable suggestion. In the past few minutes of conversation, Bash had piqued my interest more than he did earlier on. It seemed there may be a bit more to him.

"OK, a nightcap. In the bar."

"Good call, *habibti*. Let's go."

"Earlier on you asked me what I do for a living. I would like to know what you do, Vivi? What keeps you busy, what makes you happy? Where have you worked? What do you do now? I am more and more interested in you. You have a lovely, addictive quality about you. No matter how many times Theo warns me, I have a feeling that I will just not be able to let you go. I hope I will manage after we say our goodbyes but I know myself. You flipped a switch in me. And I feel we could go places together."

"You are a charmer," I smiled. "I have lived in the Levant and GCC for a great many years now. I am no longer the naïve Dutch girl. You Arabs are masters of making girls feel like there is no one else in your world. But I have got the T-shirt, Bash *habibi.*"

"I wish I could have *your* T-shirt. If I did, I would put it around my pillow and inhale your scent at night."

"How do you think of all this dross to say?" I teased him. "How about we spend the next five minutes in normal conversation without ridiculous innuendos or flirtations? Do you think you can last that long? Personally, I have my doubts. Don't get me wrong. I am charmed by you. You are a hell of a kisser. But I can't quite work out what else you are. Let's try this. Are you up to the challenge?"

"OK, I agree. And if I make it through five minutes. I get to kiss you for five. Deal?"

"I don't think there is any chance of that, but if you manage, I will gladly kiss you."

"Good. I will pretend we are meeting for the first time again and that anything that occurred earlier never happened. Is that alright?"

"Yes. Go for it, Mr. Stud! I will count you down. Three, two, one, launch!"

Bash stood up and walked away. I smiled. *What was he up to?* He turned around and walked towards me, pretending that I was seeing him for the first time. He looked hesitant at first, as if he weren't sure about approaching me.

With his head in a questioning stance, Bash looked at me and said, "Is that you Vivika? My goodness, it has been a long time. How lovely to see you!"

He came closer and took both my hands in his, leaving a polite space between us. There was warmth. He didn't crowd me out.

"How have you been?" He looked at me, with genuine interest and in a respectable way. "What a tremendous surprise to see you again."

I played along with his performance but I did not feed into

his dialogue. He had to earn the kiss. He was doing better than expected.

"May I join you?" he asked.

I nodded.

"I need to tell you the truth. I have thought about you more than you can imagine over the past years. When I listen to Vivaldi's Four Seasons, I think of you Vivi. *Vivi's* Four Seasons. When I was at an exhibition of Julius Caesar in Rome. I was there for a charity event. When I read the famous words '*Veni, Vidi, Vici';* I came, I saw, I conquered, I felt a void - Vivi. All I ever wanted was to conquer you, in the most cavalier sense.

My thoughts were *Vivi, Vivi, Vivi.*

When I learnt more about one of the great French philosophers of the age of enlightenment, Le Baron de Montesquieu, who was famous in relation to the *Trias Politica* principle, all that came to my mind was *Trias Vivika.* I realised in that instant that, all those years ago, I lost what I might never have. Your name means *life*. It is etched in my mind and grooved into my heart. I hope my life will have you in it for the rest of mine, dearest Vivika. *My life.*"

He swallowed and was quiet. What had started off as a joke suddenly seemed almost solemn. The words were nonsense and Bash's performance farfetched and ridiculous, his ramblings picked up from nowhere and glued together randomly. But he was someone softer, less brash, almost vulnerable. It was Bash as I had never seen him before.

I walked over to him and hugged him. "You did great," I said.

"Just letting my words flow, without any thought. I know

it didn't make any sense. But looking at you, there now really is only one thing I want to do. And that is, to kiss you. Do I deserve your kiss Vivi?"

"Fair is fair," I said, as I pulled him into me and kissed him for what must have been much longer than five minutes.

Long, lingering loveliness.

I spent the evening with Bash though I did not sleep with him. We had a very good time. When I wanted to go back to my place, he walked me over to the Annex. It was still snowing. Large big fluffy flakes landed silently on us.

"I am so glad to have spent some time with you, Vivi. Albeit rather interrupted. Though not *coitus interruptus*, as you never allowed me to have you in the biblical sense." He grinned and continued, "Why didn't you? We are now half a century old. What stopped you?"

"It's nothing to do with age or opportunity, Bash. I am just that way. If it feels perfectly right, I do. If it doesn't, I don't. I neither question nor justify, apologise, or make excuses. It's how it is. That's me."

"You are unique Vivi. You understand and respect yourself and understand the Arab culture, where discretion is key. Your qualities will get you far if you stick with me."

"How do you mean?"

"We can't find out all the amazing things we could get up to in just three days. But I hope you will come to see me in Marbella and talk more about that museum in Jordan, and about other possible ventures. You have a great brain Vivi, a clean heart, and an understanding of Arabs. That is rare to find in a semi-Viking. Those things are important to me and my business. Maybe you would like to start a hotel on the Dead

Sea? Or be my consultant to do that. I have funds to invest and from what I have learnt over the past three days, I would like to invest in you."

"I know you would," I flirted. "Maybe someday we will come together."

Bash knew the innuendo was intended and laughed.

"Come soon. Sometimes a window of opportunity opens and you have to fly through it. Don't ask too many questions, go with the flow. Are you able to travel at short notice?"

"I can come whenever I like. I am currently working on a tourism project in the Levant. I can work from anywhere, as long as I have my laptop and an internet connection."

"If I send you a ticket, will you come and see me and do me the honour of staying with me?"

"Thanks Bash, a kind and tempting offer but I can afford a ticket. I just don't know if it is a good idea."

"If you feel uncomfortable coming alone, why don't you come with Maddie? I have a friend Zack who would love her."

"You are a rogue Bash. You know Theo fancies Maddie. Just because you are not on the best terms now, there is no need to undermine their bond. Let them be."

"She won't be able to resist Zack. But we shall see. I am not forcing anyone to do anything, I am just positioning options and temptations. If you want it, you can have it. If you don't, no hard feelings. Hope you consider the proposition Viv. If I have meetings and you don't have to work, you and Maddie can hang out. We can get together during the evenings and have some fun. The weather is nice during spring. Consider it. Have a chat with Maddie. And if you prefer to stay at a hotel, then that is easily arranged. The owner of the *Ventana Romana* is a close connection of mine. Think about it."

"I will give it some thought," I said.

With that, Bash pulled me into him.

We stood outside the Annex door, kissing in the snow.

"*Buenas noces* Vivi," he said, as he stroked my cheek. "*Espero que vengas.* I hope you come."

"Night, Bash," I said, and went up to sleep in my old dorm for the last time.

The next day, we all trickled in for brunch around eleven o'clock. The diehards had already eaten their breakfast and were predictably sleeping off their hangovers before check-out. Others had left for the airport during the night to catch their flights back to their various far flung homes across the world.

It was great as we all managed to congregate together before we had to leave; Alex, Theo, Bash, Majida, Coco or Colette - as we had now started to call her for novelty purposes, Maddie, and Lisa.

We cracked up when we saw Maria-Stefana the Yugoslavian cleaning lady talking to Theo and pointing at Maddie, clearly asking him if he had '*jiggy-jiggy*' last night. Theo walked round behind the buffet where Maria-Stefana was standing. He gave her an enormous hug which embarrassed her and at the same time seemed to please her. We waved at her and blew her kisses. She raised her hand in response while covering her mouth with the other in embarrassed delight. As her colleague came out from the kitchen, Maria-Stefana pointed to Theo, giving herself an imaginary hug as she explained the situation without words, causing great hilarity between the women as they disappeared, giggling, out of sight.

We recorded a message for Amilcar. Everyone said a line or

two and then we all grouped around for a garbled video message saying he was missed, that we planned to pop over, and for him to take care. I pressed *send*. I wanted to call but Amilcar seemed frail and I did not want to put him in a position where he might feel overwhelmed, yet I wanted him to know he was missed. Theo confirmed what I suspected all along. Amilcar was not well.

Theo promised to talk to me about it, just as soon as he had cleared it with Amilcar that he could do so.

We ate more than we intended, chatted, took pictures, exchanged numbers, promised to call, and planned a mini-Reunion where Hélène could join us too.

When we said goodbye, there were tears, kisses, smiles, as we embraced one another. I was happy to see that Bash and Theo hugged each other. I knew they would settle their differences. Almost everyone went on their separate ways.

I nipped out for a little snog with Bash before his car arrived to pick him up. He was continuing his way to Gstaad for some meetings.

"*Ismai habibti,* here are my contact details. Give me a missed call so I have your number. Talk to Maddie and come down in a week or two. Can't wait to see you in my home."

"Will try. Would love to."

With that we said our goodbyes, hugged, briefly kissed, and went on our separate ways.

I was flying back to my *lock and leave pad* in Amsterdam and I planned to check in on Hélène who would be there. I could work from anywhere and since I had options in Amsterdam and Jordan, or at my parents in the UK, I was free to move where I wished.

Maddie was going back to Germany. I had booked a car for

Maddie and me to be taken from the mountaintop to Geneva airport. We had done the beautiful train journey along the lake on the way in, as well as the cogwheel up the mountain. We had partied hard, slept late, and we wanted to use our final time together to debrief on our Reunion Experience, and a car seemed by far the best means of transportation to optimise our last hours together.

We settled into the chauffeur driven limo, the Swiss interpretation of an *Über*, and set off down the mountain. We drove past the artificial mountains nestled between the real ones. Thirty years ago, we were told that behind the fake façades there were entire hospitals built into manmade spaces inside the mountain. I could not quite get my head around what that might look like or, indeed, how true it was. You never knew with *the Swiss*.

Everything seemed possible.

We had also heard stories at the time when we were at the school that the Swiss government could blow up any bridge that gave access to the country, at the push of a button. Word had it that if the Swiss do not want a fly to come zooming in across from the French side of Lake Geneva into Switzerland, they can prevent it from doing so, protecting their borders with laser precision.

Whether it was true or not, we didn't know, but what we did know was that there was an emergency shelter in the Annex and I imagine one is in the main building too. There was a list of items that had to be kept in stock and up to date, always, including canned food and other basics. '*Like lice*', I smiled to myself as I remember Kim's comment in Mr Neuhaus' class that day we were forced to scale the steps in the snow.

In addition to the compulsory inventory, there was a gas mask for every registered person living in The Annex. Apparently, the cows, too, had gas masks in case of need.

The Swiss are quite extraordinary.

My favourite Swiss Things included their delicious chocolate, cheese fondue, amazing landscapes, wines, and mountains. Especially the mountain we have just driven down from; *Our Mountain of Love.*

Marbella Mayhem

"Seems you gave our '*Mountain of Love*' some credit for its name, dear Maddie. It looks like you and Theo had a good time," I said, smiling.

"You and Bash too, right?" Maddie asked, smiling back at me.

"Yes, we did. I don't think it is sensible to spill the beans with Theo, but Bash asked if we would like to come down and spend some days in Marbella where he lives."

"Marbella? Oh, my goodness, that is a blast from the past!"

"I know," I said. "That is where you first met Manu, right?"

"Yes, I stayed at a most fancy hotel. Can't recall the name."

"Is it by any chance the *Ventana Romana*?"

"Yes, that's it! How do you know?"

"Bash said that he would accommodate us there if we come down for a long weekend. I am tempted to go. I want you to join me. I know that Theo will probably not feel comfortable with us staying at Bash's house but if we stay at the hotel, I think he will be fine."

"I have a close friend in Marbella I am planning to visit after my return to Europe, so perhaps we can combine. Anyhow I think you need a chaperone Vivi. As you said, I am a bit more astute and you can probably do with an extra pair of eyes and ears."

"So, you'll come with me?"

"I'll think about it. Let's make it home first before we plan our next escapade, though I must say I am tempted to combine seeing my friend with some sunshine and a trip down memory lane in that famous or should I say, infamous, hotel."

"Consider it time invested Maddiebärchen. Even if Bash had not suggested we go down, it's a really good idea. I see this as an important point in our life. I am actually very serious. I think we should keep our energy and momentum going and plan our *Thinking Retreat*. We talked about how we both want to create multiple income streams. We have not had the chance to discuss our approach and ideas in detail over this weekend for obvious reasons, but it would be great to follow through and plan ahead in the Med. Marbella could be perfect."

"You have a point. A very good one. I will check in with Emmanuelle and Eshe and have some thoughts by next week. The idea is growing on me already."

We all made it back home safely. We exchanged pictures, Facebook posts and generally kept up the *Post-Reunion* vibe for a while. Eventually, we all settled back down into our own realities and day to day lives.

Bash and I connected by WhatsApp and had some harmless banter, a bit of cheeky talk, and some good chats.

'Are you coming soon?' he wrote one day. *'I certainly hope so. My buddy at the hotel owes me badly like I said. You and Maddie*

will be well looked after by him. And I intend to do the same. Tell me you are booking flights Viv?'

At that very moment I received a WhatsApp message from Maddie, 'I have been thinking, which did not take me very long. We should kick off Q2 with a plan in hand and therefore it is instrumental, necessary, and desirable that we confirm our retreat. If you are OK with Marbella, so am I. Why go somewhere else? Let's do this.'

I responded straightaway, 'Good call Mads. We don't want to look back on being doughnuts. What dates? So, I can let Bash know.'

'21st of March. First day of spring. Has to be done. Our first Income for Life Plan will be in place by April.'

I sent Bash a note, 'Result! We are coming. Mission to plan multiple income streams, to think about next twenty years, to firm up strategy and to have fun and see you. If you are up for that?'

Bash responded immediately, 'Totally up for that. Happy to hear. Consider the hotel booked 21st March through to the 26th. You can stay longer, but not shorter.' This was followed by a smiling emoji and a bright red heart.

'Only 9 days away. I am counting the minutes. Looking forward Guapa X'.

Maddie and I flew in from Frankfurt and Amsterdam respectively. It was great to see each other so soon after our Swiss Reunion. We were greeted by a driver with a sign saying, 'Ms Ulrich and Ms Baron, Hotel Ventana Romana'. The driver took our luggage and we settled into the limo.

"Good old Bash. He started off well!"

"Indeed, he did Viv. He is redeeming himself in my eyes, though I must admit I am a bit uncomfortable that Theo doesn't know we are here."

"I feel the same Mads, but you and I are plotting and planning our future. Anything or anyone else is additional. Our main purpose of being here is entirely business related."

"That is how I am justifying our being here. Though I also question why I need to *justify* my presence. Theo is a great guy and in my heart of hearts I feel I am cheating on him, which is a bit confusing since we are not in a relationship. We just had fun."

"Let's remember we are here for ourselves and for each other. And everything else will fall into place, I am sure of it."

On arrival at the hotel Bash was waiting for us. He embraced us both. He didn't treat me any differently to Maddie, which was good.

"Sorry I could not be at the airport but, rest assured, I will be at your beck and call whenever you need or want anything. Let us settle you into your suites and make sure you are looked after and that you ladies can relax before anything else."

As we went into the lobby, we were greeted by the General Manager, "Welcome to the *Ventana Romana,* ladies. We hope you have a wonderful stay. My name is Claus and here is my card in case you need anything at all. I am at your service."

"Thank you, Claus," Maddie and I both said, in unison.

Bash caught the attention of a guy walking towards us. He was *drop-dead-gorgeous*. I could see Maddie doing a double take, too.

"Allow me to introduce you to my business partner and friend, Zack. He is the man behind this lovely property and has solemnly sworn he will take the most exquisite care of you."

"Hello ladies and welcome to your Marbella home. Bash is my brother. And I am your host, but hopefully we can become friends. Anything you need or wish for or anything your heart desires, please call me. Here is my number. I am privileged to have you staying with us. If you allow Bash and me to invite you to dinner tonight, it will be our great honour."

"Thank you, that will be wonderful," I said.

"Utterly lovely," Maddie added.

Bash was smiling. We all were. The arrival experience was great. I hoped that the rest of the week would pan out well too.

"It's 3pm now girls. How does 8pm for dinner sound? We will pick you up but wear something warm. It might be chilly on deck."

"Sounds great, see you later," we said and were escorted to our rooms.

"Blimey, he was a bit of a looker Mads," I said.

"What a handsome specimen," Maddie agreed. "Probably not nearly as cavalier in real life. It's just not possible that good looking, wealthy and genuine, go together in one package. He is certainly easy on the eye. But the last time I gave in to '*easy on the eye*', was when I met Manu here. And that was an experience that is hard to forget or ignore. Let us take it easy and concentrate on our things, our business streams and our future."

"Fully agree. It's really nice to be here, but we need to be here on our terms."

We had interconnecting suites. I knew that Bash had arranged for us to have our own space, yet at the same time be close to each other.

"How gorgeous. What a pad. It's like the penthouse, but with separating doors between wings. Bless you Bash and thank you, *Mr. Handsome*. What was his name? Dick?"

"No, Mads; Zack."

"Ah, a Berliner moment. Sorry Buss."

"No worries. How about we take an hour or so to unpack and have a shower or bath, and then open our interconnecting palaces and order tapas and *Cava* up to the terrace?"

"The last time I saw the view from over the Med from this vantage point was when I was sitting opposite Manu on the first day, I met him. Twenty years ago."

"Wow, Maddie. You have already had an entire adventure in this place. I wonder what will happen next."

We checked out each other's rooms and then went our own ways for the next hour.

Both suites were identical in size with all mod-cons and luxuries in place. The vase of fragrant white roses stood next to the bucket with Champagne on ice. Hand-made truffles in white, milk, dark chocolate with hot pepper and strawberry were carefully placed on a round antique table near the French windows. The doors opened on to our shared terrace.

I popped a few chocolates in my mouth and then indulged in a soak in the bath with a glass of Cava. I always made it a habit to thank my lucky stars when I was in these fortunate situations and I did so again in my amazing suite in the *Ventana Romana*, blissfully unaware of what was yet to come.

After an hour, as agreed, we opened our interconnecting doors and took our papers, staples, tape, and notebooks outside on to the spacious terrace.

"I am going to call for a flip chart. Do we need anything else?"

"Double sided tape, so we can hang the pages up and have a clear overview."

Within fifteen minutes we had the tools we needed.

"What income streams can we tap into," Maddie asked, holding a marker in one hand, standing in front of the flip chart, as if she were teaching.

"You look the part, Mads. I can imagine you instructing a gaggle of hotel students."

She laughed, "Let's perform a little SWOT on ourselves. Let's just throw our strengths, weakness, opportunities, and threats out there. If you write them down, we can do a structural review, just like we would do in any job. If we get stuck, we can call out each other's weaknesses and strengths. Sometimes it's easier for someone else to see what you can't."

"OK, here we go," Maddie says. "Strengths are internal qualities. One obvious strength is that we both know about different cultures. We both travelled a lot, we know how to lead teams, how to organise events, what it takes to set up a business, how to manage money and we have a strong network in the industry. Anything else?"

"We have creative minds, we have learnt from past mistakes, we hate politics, we cannot abide fools, we see opportunity where others may not, we are bold, adventurous."

"Do you think not abiding fools is a strength or a weakness?" Maddie wondered.

"I think if you put up with fools you are undermining yourself, so yes a strength."

"Put like that, I agree."

"Now let's have some fun with the weaknesses. Again, weaknesses need to be assessed from an internal perspective. What do we have Buss?"

"We don't abide fools, so that characteristic fits into both categories."

157

"We are both low on finances, we can't stay in one place for long, we don't live in the same country, we don't yet have a plan," I added.

"Hm. That's a bit depressing. We better pour a glass of bubbly to lift our spirits," Maddie reflected.

I filled our glasses.

"As for the opportunities," I said, to continue our project. "We know from experience what our gaps in terms of education are since we lived through both school and work. If I were running a hotel management education programme, I would actively teach *cultural awareness*. Between us, we know about Europe, Middle East, and Africa. Even though many hotel schools have a great number of nationalities, it is different when you set out into the business world. For example, in the Middle East you must never show the sole of your foot. It is disrespectful. Once there was a new Ambassador who came to Jordan and put his feet up on the table as he started his team meeting. Everyone walked out and the guy had no idea what he'd done wrong. It is that simple. He had offended the very team he was trying to engage, through his unfortunate ignorance. Another example would be if you go into a lift in the Middle East. You should find a place against the wall. If it is too busy and you are forced to take a central position in the elevator, you must excuse your back. Those are just two examples. If students and expats know these things, they can fare much better. I am sure you have similar situations across Africa. And even within Europe as we discussed in the past, with our multi-cultural parents, expectations are different. So, this may be an opportunity."

We looked at each other and agreed that we might be on to something.

I sipped on my drink and continued, "How about if we design a training course for hotel management students and international business students, who are aiming to work in the world of international hospitality or business. We could teach in person and develop short clips of impactful, funny, and poignant situations, catching the attention of the student through engagement and intuitive understanding. They would then learn lessons that serve as eye openers that they will never forget and will save them from avoidable disaster."

Maddie added, "And, perhaps teach their children and educate the next generation of more astute and respectful citizens, whether they are related to international hotels or not. Building understanding, respect and intercultural bridges."

"Let's work this out and, without giving too much away and let us test the principle on Zack tonight. I don't think Bash will be interested but Zack might be. He is after all the man behind this hotel, or so Bash says, and he may be a good sounding board for our idea in principle. That will be an insightful session. Imagine what we can achieve when we put our minds to it. Am happy we came. We kicked off our stay well."

"I fully agree. Shall we go for a swim and a suntan before dinner?" Maddie suggested.

"Let's do it."

By 7.45 pm and after what we considered a fruitful afternoon, we had showered and got dressed. I was wearing my long dress with turquoise and tangerine swirls that I loved; I had worn it in some interesting scenarios in the past. I particularly remember the meeting with General Salim in Dubai. I wondered how he was doing as I had not been in touch with him for a while.

Maybe I should let sleeping dogs lie.

Maddie wore a white linen dress with a tan belt and espadrilles. We were about to leave the suite when I recalled Bash saying to bring something warm. I grabbed a funky little cardigan and my pashmina that worked well over the dress and Maddie took her oversized merino wool cream scarf. When we came downstairs, Bash and Zack were waiting for us.

"*Hola guapas,*" Bash greeted us.

"You both look stunning," Zack said.

Then I spotted another guy who was looming in the background. "Nick, come on over and be introduced," Zack said to him.

Nick came towards us and shook hands. "How do you do?"

"How do you do?" both Maddie and I answered.

Only the Brits would ask a question then to answer it with the same question, as it is etiquette.

Zack continued, "Nick is the marvellous man who sails our yacht. Nick, Bash, and I, are friends and business partners, *The Golden Triangle*. We wanted you to meet so you can go off sailing whenever you like. The yacht is docked here in the harbour at *Puerto Banus*. We thought it might be nice to go out on the water for some bubbly and tapas. That way you know where to go when you fancy a sail. There is a full moon tonight. I have some extra, freshly laundered, blankets so you won't get cold."

"Sounds great," I smiled.

"Love the idea," Maddie concurred and off we set.

We were greeted with a glass of Champagne as we boarded. Zack invited us to take a seat round the beautiful wooden, built-in table. We sank into the sumptuous navy cushions with a white trim and started chatting.

Very naval.

Bash took a seat next to me. Zack sat next to Maddie.

"We will go out on the engine this evening but whenever you are up for some plain sailing, let me know," Nick said.

Nick was charming and reminded me in a small way of Captain James who was no longer alive. I looked up to heaven and send him my love.

Nick set off to start the engines to take us out onto the moonlit waters of the Med.

"Bash tells me you ladies are high flying hospitality professionals. He proclaims you are the best, most creative and determined women he knows," Zack said.

"Cheers, Bash, what a lovely message to convey. Much appreciated," I said.

Maddie raised her glass. "Lovely to be here. Thank you for having us."

We all raised our glasses. "Thank you for gracing us with your presence," Zack said.

The crew who offered us Champagne on arrival, made regular appearances to keep our glasses topped up and placed exquisite style tapas on the table in front of us. The tapas were different. A quail egg topped off with some caviar, a grilled olive and *percebes.*

I had not eaten these barnacles since the trade fair in Madrid many moons ago. I recalled my time there with Othman a colleague from the Middle East, with whom I had a fling for a while. He was the same person who made my first trip to Dubai, beyond memorable. After a day of intensive work at the travel trade fair, *Fitur*, we used to get together for dinner. Our favourite place was the upscale restaurant *Paradis*, right across from the hotel where we were staying.

In the centre of the starched white tablecloths, covering round tables, a solitary apple was placed. Each apple was branded with a 'P'. This was achieved by placing a paper cut out of the letter on its peel before it was left to ripen. The part of the apple exposed to the sun became a deeper shade, allowing the 'P' for *Paradis* to stand out. It was a creative alternative to a floral arrangement and much more cost effective and memorable too.

It was during one of these meals at Paradis when I first ate *'percebes'* known as *goose barnacles*. They are considered a delicacy from Galicia in the northwest of Spain and they are among the most exclusive seafoods in the world. The best quality percebes will sell to the Portuguese and Spanish for around two hundred euros in current currency. I remembered my sales manager at the time, Marta, who was from Galicia, explaining why this food was so expensive. Apart from it being delicious, the way the barnacles are harvested is dangerous. Marta told us that the people who harvest percebes, are dropped by rope from the cliffs above to land on slippery rocks that are pounded by the Atlantic waves. Then, when the wave retreats, the percebes harvesters must cut the tough dinosaur shaped claws off the slippery rocks and then they are hoisted up above the pounding of the sea before the next wave comes smashing onto the rocks again. The place of harvest was called Costa da Morte, The Coast of Death.

If you got your timing wrong, you might pay for it with your life.
I took a barnacle and looked at Bash.

"Have you had these babies before?" he asked.

"Yes, I have, quite a long time ago. Even though I know how to eat them, removing the little flat shell at the top of them first, I already know what to expect."

"What is that?" he asked.

"You know what I mean," I replied.

"Is it because they sometimes seem to ejaculate as you put them in your mouth and they explode?"

"Exactly. When you pull the tubular shaped piece out of its little cylinder, sometimes the juice starts flying. Not sure if it is the trapped water or what, but yes it looks like something out of a blue movie."

Zack started laughing, "Ejaculate away girls with your perce-bes. We do the same all the time. Don't worry. You are amongst friends. Salud!"

He raised his glass and we toasted again.

"All this toasting and cheering reminded me of the *Scandi Clan* at school. The Vikings were always drinking Aquavit and every two minutes you would find yourself saying '*skoll*' *and* downing the next shot. They really knew how to get a party going. They just didn't have any idea when to stop but they are good fun," I recalled.

"Sounds like you had quite a blast at that school. Its repu-tation in the international world of hospitality is very strong indeed. I lead on various hotels and I will be instructing my management to take on staff who have been trained at your institution. They clearly are responsible for high quality, intelligent and creative professionals, as per my evidence-based observation," said Zack. He raised his glass again to us and then he winked at Bash. "Bash is not great at running a hotel but he excels in terms of his appreciation of art. In all its forms."

"Talking of art, I stayed in your gorgeous property some twenty years ago," Maddie said. "I was working in Addis and oversaw opening a new luxury hotel. I love art and the management of my hotel sent me here to attend an art exhibition."

"That is extraordinary," Zack responded. "You mean I could have made your acquaintance some twenty years ago? What a wasted opportunity, though I am delighted to meet you both now."

"Do you know an artist by the name of Jacques? He was one of the painters whose art we bought. He already seemed to be in his seventies at the time."

"Dear Jacques," Zack said. "He was a brilliant painter. He had an excellent eye. Especially where beauty was concerned. He had a distinct appreciation of the masculine. I remember him telling me about a model, from Addis I think, strangely enough, who he had tried to hook into his net but he hadn't managed it. Sadly, Jacques passed away, but his paintings continue to give joy and increase in value as time goes by."

"I am sorry to hear that Jacques passed away. And, as for that male model you are talking about, I happen to know that he too is dead." Maddie said.

I was shocked to hear Maddie be so definitive about Manu. But also relieved. For Maddie, Manu was no more. That chapter was closed. She considered him *morto*.

We had a great evening talking about hospitality and antiquities, mosaics, and frescoes.

"These are a few of my favourite things," I said.

"You do strike me more as an '*Out of Africa*' girl, rather than

'*The Sound of Music*'," said Nick who had now joined us, having left one of the crew to steer the yacht.

"I love both films but it is Maddie who is the *African Queen*, I am closer with the Middle East."

"I was based in Jordan for a little while during the Iraqi War," Nick continued. "An extraordinary place. Such a rich cultural heritage. I loved it there."

"Were you there for work?" Maddie asked Nick.

"Yes, I was. Can't say too much about that, though what I can say is that I could see great possibilities in Jordan. It is said that all these years later it has not yet taken off. For tourism, yes, but economically speaking it is still struggling. The weather is so incredible there and the people so hospitable, but really it is tourism that is the ace they have up their sleeve."

"Nick, you never told me your point of view on hospitality in Jordan before," Zack said.

"I can't recall you asking me about that particular subject, country, or angle," Nick laughed. "But yes, I do think that Jordan is a spectacular country."

"Though it is not economically resilient as you say," Zack continued. "Do you think it would align with our business? Maybe you, Bash, and I, should think along those lines. We are ready to expand our investments. I believe in fate and opportunity and I think having these amazing, well experienced ladies with us, may give us opportunities to discuss."

"Cheers to that Zack," Bash said. "Let's reignite the opportunities that the early silk traders capitalised on. The Silk Road and the Spice Route are the ancient trading veins. They still serve us today but can perhaps be made more efficient. Are you open to that suggestion, ladies?"

"Always open to discuss," I responded.

Maddie nodded in agreement, "We can always have a think session and see."

"Sounds like a plan," Zack said. "Nick how about we go back home for a cup of our famous, or should I say, infamous, hot cocoa? It is getting chilly. We can get together tomorrow or the day after, whenever suits. I don't want to take your time or cramp your style, but I can see there are avenues to explore, if you think so too."

"Sounds good," I agreed.

"Great idea," Maddie added, as Nick got up to steer the yacht back to shore and in to port.

Marshmallow Musings

When we returned to the hotel Maddie and I thanked Bash, Zack, and Nick, for a great evening out. Bash said he would be in touch over the next day or two, to discuss business.

"I can understand you would like to relax but allow me to send you up some hot chocolate before bed," Zack said.

We accepted his kind offer, said goodnight, and parted ways.

"I am going to jump under the shower. Shall we share a cup of cocoa on the terrace before bed?"

"Good call, Buss. See you when it arrives."

The hot chocolate experience was one I was not going to forget.

Two hand painted mugs arrived, delightfully decorated with Andalusian geometric patterns. They sat side by side on a hand-made wooden tray that was inlaid with mother of pearl.

Two freshly starched napkins appeared elegant yet plain until you detected a beautiful detail that ran along one side of the napkin, like a henna tattoo, in the same Arabesque pattern.

The stirrers were sticks that had heads of brown crystallised sugar. They were laid out neatly next to the silver spoons which boasted the same geometric pattern running up their handles.

Large chunks of chocolate were piled up in another dish.

"Gosh, how divine," I gasped.

"Exquisite," Maddie agreed, as she started grating the rocks of chocolate indulgence into submission. As she did, the rich shavings created a pile on the plate provided for that purpose.

"I have not yet decided who is playing which role and what their plan is."

"How do you mean?" I asked, as I lifted the gleaming thermos and poured the hot frothy milk into the cups.

"These guys are up to something Buss. They are charming but my radar is picking up on an underlying vibe."

Maddie put the shavings into the hot milk. The chocolate melted, colouring, and flavouring the milk.

"What's under that little Moroccan looking silver dish? More hidden temptations to sweeten us up?" I asked, as I lifted the lid from the container to find handmade mini marshmallows of different shapes. "These boys certainly know their way into a woman's heart, don't they?" I popped a handful of baby mallows into my full cup of milk, creating a little mountain on top of the froth.

Maddie carefully selected three mini marshmallows from the handcrafted silver container and, as she dropped them into the sweet concoction, one by one, she said, "Nick. Zack. Bash." Then she put her cane-sugar swizzle stick into the milk and stirred it all up.

"We need to treat these men with caution, Viv. They are up to something."

It all felt rather ominous to me.

We said goodnight and went off to bed. However, I tossed

and turned, unable to sleep much. What Maddie said was playing around in my brain for most of the night. In my mind, the purpose of this trip was to think about future business streams for Maddie and me and to enjoy time with Bash. I was open to explore if he and I had any potential. But after this evening's musings from Maddie, I was thinking differently about everything.

The next morning, I woke up early. I got up and sat on the large wicker chair on the terrace having fixed myself a coffee. I hugged my pulled up knees, looking out over the Med. My palms felt the heat of the liquid through my mug as I clasped it. I could feel the morning sunshine on my face making my cheeks gently throb. I always found the spring sunshine to be a joy. The first rays after the cold weather of winter were a welcome arrival, but they were stronger than you might think. If you weren't careful, the March sunshine could easily burn the unsuspecting, exposed skin that had just re-appeared after months of hibernation.

After some time, Maddie appeared. She had her coffee in her hand. Maddie had not slept much either.

"Do you think we are reading too much badness into the situation?", I asked her. "Maybe we came home in the dark yesterday and perhaps your memories of this place gave you a bad feeling about good people Mads. On this bright morning, I can't quite imagine there is anything dubious going on. I think Bash is a good guy in essence. And as Zack is associated, he is probably all good too."

"Bussi with both my deepest love and respect, you know that you always see the best in people. And sometimes perhaps you see the illusion of good. But not everyone is as you imagine or would like them to be. There are opportunists out there, scammers, frauds, and conmen. Of course, there are genuine people too. When we were on the mountain, we were all still growing up and finding our way. But thirty years later you can see the personalities, how they have taken on their true form.

When I found you again, I knew that you were still the person who was my friend then and would be forever. But others have chosen their paths. And though they don't think so, it is easy enough to read them. If you just probe. And listen. However, for you, it is a new angle as you are not prone to mistrust. The difference between trusting and questioning people you like, is not natural in your case. For me, I have been questioning and doubting the person I loved, let alone the people I liked, for the past decades. And it has served me well in the end. It takes some time and I got burned along the way. I can see trouble, though it is not yet clear what it may be nor unravelled or in focus. Let us call it a strong hunch for now."

I thought about what Maddie had said.

"I have to say, Mads, even though I am very happy to see Bash, my tummy did not do a flip when I saw him here in Spain. It was kind of a 'take it or leave it' feeling. Even on the yacht, with Bash sitting next to me, I was very comfortable, so there was nothing uneasy there. He sat with his arm around the back of my head, playing with my hair. But his presence doesn't drive me nuts, making me want to leave with him and get off the yacht to dive into bed. And to be fair, there appeared no urgency from his side either."

"I know he likes you, Buss. There is no doubt in my mind that he would be delighted to spend the next days with you frolicking in bed on the Med. The reason I think both of you seem to be feeling this way is because there is a bigger thing going on. More important than us. More important than Bash's fun or pleasure and having a great time with you. If you feel comfortable, play along. Just be you and let me be the eyes and ears. I will share my findings and if I may, give you directions, as this game, or mission of theirs, evolves."

"Jeez, Mads, you sound like an undercover agent."

"I have had plenty of practice, especially recently when I was planning and plotting my escape from Ethiopia and away from Manu. Check this out."

Maddie opened her handbag on the chair next to her and took out a pen.

I was intrigued. "What is so special about that pen? Does it symbolise us writing our next chapter in life, or does it mean we will be signing great contracts in our mutual business going forward?"

"No, my favourite Berliner. None of that. Look," she answered, as she passed me the pen.

I glanced at it. "So, it's a pen."

"Yes. Correct. Though it is more than a pen. It is a recording spy pen."

"What the hell, Mads! Are you mad? Where did all this paranoia come from?"

"Not paranoia, my friend. I am just a bit more experienced than you. Unfortunately. But when matters went belly up with Manu, he banned me from having my phone with me. In case I recorded our conversations with the plan to implicate him. Not that I needed much more evidence. Anyhow I got my sister from Germany to send me a few recorder pens, which she forwarded to my company mail at the hotel. I always used those pens at work and at home, and as they were around all the time, they did not raise suspicion. The snippets I recorded helped me to speed up my divorce, which is now in the pipeline. Without the evidence, it would still be his word against mine. In a patriarchal society, being a female, that is dangerous. In our current situation we are dealing with men who are slick, savvy and street smart. They are charming, handsome, engaging, and dangerous as sin, if you ask me."

"Wow. I don't know what to say. More importantly I don't know what to do. Should we avoid them?"

"On the contrary *Mata Hari*. You stay true to who you are, with your bubbly conversation and enthusiasm. You know Bash is fascinated by your Mayan amulet. He mentioned art and said he is interested in talking to that archaeologist in Jordan, as you told me when we were on the mountain. Zack called their little team *The Golden Triangle*. We will call them that too, making them believe we repeat what they say and that we don't think for ourselves or question their remarks. Between you and me, we must see them as *The Bermuda Triangle* also dubbed *The Devil's Triangle*, where things and people disappear in mysterious circumstances."

Maddie took a sip of her orange juice and continued, "You engage them Buss. Be the talkative one. I will listen, note, and record. Don't worry about me. I will use my pen with the bright pink plaster on it. If anyone asks, I'll say it is holding the pen together. It's my lucky one that broke and I fixed it with a bright splash of fluorescent pink, in the form of a kid's plaster. I can record anything without coming under suspicion. You know the principle. You are bubbly. I am quiet. Say anything you like, flirt with Bash if you want to, snog him if you guys feel like it. He is superficial in conversation but it will relax him and make him think that you believe in him. Think about it. If you had to choose between Bash or Theo. Who would you trust?"

"Theo. Without a shadow of a doubt," I replied.

"You already knew that Bash was a bit suspect and in your heart of hearts, that was why you did not sleep with Bash when you could have done so on the mountain. It was I expect, also the reason why you did not drop Theo a line, saying that you and I were going for some fun in the sun at Bash's place."

"You are right, Mads. I must admit that I am worried about what Theo might say or do and do not want drama. But he seems to be concerned about something as it relates to Bash and he does not want him near either of us. Though we are both here."

"But we know that we are on a mission, to find out what the hell their plan is. They have realised I think that you and I can lead them to source markets and networks, where we have trusted contacts and where they can by association with us, make quick wins, and then get out."

"Give me some bubbles please, Maddiebärchen. This orange juice could do with becoming a *Mimosa*. If I understand you correctly, we need to appear normal but think with our mission in mind."

"Exactly girlfriend, let's give those Bermuda Boys a run for their money."

"There is one thing. I don't trust them; I think we should pay for our rooms. I don't want to take advantage of them."

"Oh, my dear lord, Buss, you are utterly useless. You would immediately cause suspicion. Now who is the doughnut? I know Bash at least likes us. But put it into your head, they can exploit us by giving us a false sense of security by paying for our room and taking care of our every whim. As far as I am concerned, we are simply applying equality. We show them we like them too, though we will not allow ourselves to be exploited."

Consultants & Conmen

"I'll get it," I said, as the phone rang.

"Hi Bash, top of the morning to you. How are you? Thanks for last night. It was nice to go out on the sea and to spend time with you, Zack and Nick."

Maddie waved at me.

"Maddie says, hi."

In response I waved at Maddie, "Hi, from Bash."

I listened to Bash speaking and responded, "Consulting? For a glamp-site in Morocco? Wow, that's quite a message first thing in the morning. Thanks for thinking of us. I will run it by Maddie. Let's meet for coffee if that works for you. Sure, in an hour should be OK."

"What was that?" Maddie asked.

"That was our charming blond Arab, *Bashikins*. He said that Zack was impressed by us two *Power Women* and that he wants to engage us, fully paid, over the next few days to see what we think about his Glamping Project in Morocco."

"Are you messing with me, Bussi?"

"That's pretty much what Bash told me. It all seems a bit

unlikely, but Bash said he would talk about the details over coffee. He asked if the idea resonated in principle. What do you think, Maddie?"

"Hm. I don't know. Are they playing us? What are they up to? I really have no idea what to think Viv. I recommend we go for coffee and learn a bit more about what is going on."

"I told Bash we can meet him downstairs in an hour. Is that alright with you?"

"Bring it on I say. Let's have some fun with this. As long as we don't get burned Buss."

"Should we come up with some code language?"

"Just keep your cool and be yourself Viv. But when I mention *'Berliner',* hold fire, and pay attention to the direction we need to go. If you are alert, and don't get carried away, it will be seamless. We can only practice in real life. We will be fine. And who knows, we can start our first baby income stream in our quest for wealth from multiple sources."

An hour later, Maddie and I were in the lobby. Bash arrived looking dapper and if the truth be told ridiculously attractive. *That was a bit of a worry, but hey ho.*

"Ciao, Bella Donne; Good morning, lovely ladies," Bash greeted us.

Not sure why he was chattering in Italian while in Spain, I responded, *"Hola guapo,"* and gave him a lingering hug, making sure that my bosoms touched his torso.

"Well, a very good morning to you too, *habibti*, what a lovely start to the day."

Maddie shot me a glance as if to ask what I was playing at.

"Let me organise some coffee and juices. Do you feel like anything in particular?"

"I am good with anything, thank you Bash," Maddie responded.

"I would love a *jugo de Piña* and a *cortado,* if that's OK?"

"Sure, that is OK, *Guapa.* I like a girl who tells me what she wants so I can arrange it for her."

Bash could have waited for the server to come to us, instead he went over to arrange the order.

"What the hell, Buss?" Maddie asked.

"I am taking a leaf out of Mata Hari's book. I read up on her. She was seductive, Dutch, and she got what she wanted in terms of information. As far as I can make out, anyway. I speed-read her history and can only remember the words: *'erotica, spy, French, German, and many divorces'.* One way or another, I am going to step up my game and apply them to our situation."

"You utter nutter, Viv! This is not some sort of a play or theatre performance. These guys, as far as I can see, are pretty savvy and determined."

"I thought you said I could be flirty with Bash. He seemed to like it; don't you think?"

"Yes, he clearly did. For goodness' sake though, don't exaggerate girlfriend. We don't want to let them know we are on to something."

"You gave me permission to be a ditsy with Bash. And at the same time, you will keep me on the path when you give me the Berliner code word. So, I am prepared. I have a sneaky feeling this may turn out to be a very different kind of a break from what we'd expected."

At that moment Bash returned. "Coffee is on its way, lovely ladies. I ordered a brandy with them to oil the day, though

I must say I am delighted with my welcome which did not require any oiling at all."

He came over to me and slid his arm around my waist. I took his face between my hands and kissed him fully on the lips. "Thank you for being such a total *caballero.* You Arabs are real men. Not like some others."

"Well, thank you *habibti,* Vivi. You understand the male psyche and the Arab way. That is rare to find and I appreciate it. But I mentioned that to you before."

When Bash wasn't looking Maddie fixed her eyes on me as if to say, '*Enough already, what are you up to?'*

I knew her well enough to know that she was also enjoying this nonsensical performance and my little act. I liked Bash, don't get me wrong. If I didn't, I would never have been able to flirt with him. But I was having fun. Why not? Fun in the sun.

Make the most of any situation and if you can create great memories, then go ahead and enjoy it.

After we settled into our coffees, juices and morning brandies, Zack arrived. He didn't waste any time.

"Ladies, we are privileged to have you in our presence. I can't believe God's Grace has brought you here. As it happens, I am about to take over a Luxury Camp in Morocco and I don't have the time nor the creative ability to see its full potential. I want to ask if you would agree to flying out there later today to discuss the proposed project with the owner-manager. Going to Morocco would take too long but you can meet him in Ronda where he has another similar camp which is also included in the proposition, though naturally very different from the desert camp. He is going through a divorce and needs to move the business on. Unfortunate for him but good for us perhaps, as we have managed to negotiate him down to 45% BMV."

I knew the abbreviation meant *Below Market Value*. If Maddie didn't know, she did not let on.

Zack continued, "If you can go and do a high level quick and dirty feasibility study for us, we will pay you a respectable sum for taking you away from the pool and any other plans you may have. How does that sound?"

Normally I would have jumped at it in my enthusiasm, but I kept calm and let Maddie lead the way. I noticed that she was holding the pen with the fluorescent pink plaster on it. *OMG she's spying already*, I thought to myself, with a sense of purpose and excitement.

"Actually, Vivika and I are here for other reasons and are not in the position to sit around the pool and lounge about. We are delighted to be able to work from here and it is so lovely to spend time with you gentlemen, but I am afraid we have bigger fish that have to be fried."

Both Zack and Bash looked momentarily taken aback and, just as quickly, they recovered.

"Of course," Zack said. "Please forgive me. It was insensitive and short sighted of me to think you had leisure time to spare. I don't know if you would be agreeable to a sum of ten thousand euros each for forty eight hours of your time. I know money is not the most important factor. If you could see your way to accommodating us, we would be most humbly appreciative."

"Thank you, Zack, for your rationale. We appreciate you sharing your thoughts. As you say, the funds are not the obstacle. Your financial offer is acceptable though Vivika and I must convene and let you know whether it is a proposition we can agree to. We, like you, expect the best results. That goes for when we engage people, as well as when we are engaged. Can we give you a decision by one o'clock?"

"Thank you, Maddie. Yes, of course. I hope you can confirm ladies but respect your decision should you decide to decline. Though as I said, I hope you will accept our proposition." At that moment, Zack was given a message from the concierge. He excused himself and left.

Bash stayed with us and finished his coffee and brandy. "You make me proud, you two," he said.

"Why is that?" I asked.

"You don't put up with Zack's B.S. You push back. He is a friend but he is also a bully. Anyone who is not strong enough will be royally exploited by him. You held your ground and that is good. I must love you and leave you. Let me know what you decide and whatever it is, it is entirely up to you."

Bash came over to me and said, "Can I see you later for a catch up, or as soon as you get back, if you decide to go?"

"Sure," I replied. "I look forward to that."

Bash left.

I looked at Maddie. "How did that go, detective?"

"Not bad. I was a bit worried in the beginning that you were being gullible and girly, but I think you were playing the game, not too badly I might add," Maddie replied.

"Ten thousand euro per person for forty eight hours work and you almost spat in his face," I said.

"If you act like you have a dick but they know you own a pussy, you can get away with murder Bussi."

We both crack up, laughing.

"Let's go for a dip in the pool and make a decision. Whether we are in or out," I suggested.

"Do you think we should be *Conmen Consultants*?" Maddie asked.

"It certainly brings in more money than an 8am - 11pm in hospitality does. I wonder why we worked like dogs for peanuts."

At one o'clock, or just after, I called Bash.

"Bash, thanks for the opportunity, but we don't think it is worth the effort for that amount of money. The deal we stand to lose over the next forty eight hours will weigh heavier. Thanks for the thought, but we are not able to do the feasibility study."

It is quiet on the other end of the line. "What if we double the funds and halve the time. Can you fit it in then?"

"Why are you so keen for Maddie and me to look at the Camp. Surely it's not rocket science?"

"It isn't Viv, but a lot rides on it. An awful lot. I can't say more than that."

Maddie was listening in on the other phone. She gave a thumbs up.

"*Isma, habibi Bash,* if it matters a lot to you, Maddie and I will do it. Let Zack double the money and we won't halve the time. Does that sound like an agreeable compromise?"

"Fair, my darling Viv. That sounds more than reasonable. Zack should pay for excellence. You are exquisite. The only thing I am bummed about is that Zack will want you to leave soonest. When are you and I going to have '*We Time*?'"

"Don't worry about that. We will be back soon and have time to play."

"I will send some warm fleeces and jackets as it gets cold at night. I know you are not too far away but you won't be in a hotel. You will have two phones preloaded and charged with my number on speed dial. It there is anything at all you need, be sure to call me. I want you to be safely returned to me."

"OK thanks. We are ready. Please tell Zack that we need the full amount up front. That is our policy. Any job that we take on needs to be paid upfront within 72 hours and this job will be starting within an hour or two."

"No problem, Viv. Understood. Is cash alright for you?"

"Sure, will I see you before we go?"

"Yes, I will have the clothes brought up to your room as well as the phones and the funds. I will steal a kiss before I go if you allow me."

"I will totally allow you, darling Bash," I said. "See you later blond boy." Then I hung up.

Maddie was sitting in the deep blue velvet chair, the colour of the ocean. She looked at me with her mouth open, her big brown eyes practically popping out of her head.

"What?" I ask, feigning surprise.

"Your performance just now was epic. You are a hell of a quick learner Viv. I am beyond impressed. You just doubled the budget and got them to practically beg us to do the job."

"I am just having fun. If you are not particularly vested in a thing, it means you can be more chilled out and with that comes more oxygen. It's not a scientific approach but, hey, if we get our *pesetas,* then we will have enough euros to last the next three months. That will allow us to work out our business proposition to teach cultural awareness courses with impact in hospitality institutions worldwide."

"Class act girl. You killed it!"

Bash

Bash sent up some warm clothes and Timberlands in the right size to our suites.

We were both shoe size 39, but how did he know?

He included some warm socks, fleeces, two fully charged latest iPhones with his three numbers on them already, as well as a large box of chocolates, two bottles of fine wine, and one bottle of Champagne. Bash also included a pair of Gucci sunglasses for Maddie and some Tiffany shades for me.

Mine had a little message in my Tiffany blue holster; it reads: '*Come back to me soon and have breakfast with me. It may not be at Tiffany's, but we will do that soon. You are a gem, Viv. I think I am falling for you.*'

"Maddie. Help!" I showed her the note.

"Oh no, Viv. How are we to know if it is true or not? Is he playing our game? Are you playing a game, or do you have feelings for him, or does he for you?"

"I don't know, Mads. The whole thing is disturbing, exciting, confusing, and most likely, even dangerous. Perhaps we'd best just keep our cool and strip out any emotion and get the job done. This is to assess the potential of the luxury camp from the current owner and deliver an overview and a broad brush feasibility review. Then Zack can decide whether he wants to integrate it into his portfolio. I don't know whether this proposition involves Bash in any way. However, Bash is categorically clear that a lot is riding on this. We don't have any visibility on what that means. Our job is straightforward. They delivered the funds in cash. Now let us deliver our part of the bargain."

"Where did you put the money, Viv?"

"I told reception not to allow anyone into our room for cleaning while we are away. I stuffed the cash in the toilet cistern, having bled it dry first. It just about fitted, but I had to stuff the piles of notes in. They may not look so pristinely fresh and crisp when we fish them out of the tank, though they won't have lost their purchase power or intrinsic value."

A look of utter disbelief spread across Maddie's face. "You put the cash in the cistern tank?"

"Yes. I wrapped the stacks of notes very well in plastic first. I used the bags we got in duty-free. I took the sanitary bags from all the bathrooms, tore off the plastic protection that was slipped over the bathrobes after laundry, and took the slippers out of their plastic covers. I used all those waterproof wrappings from around the room. I naturally was not going to let that stash of cash disintegrate in the toilet flushing water. I switched off the taps that filled the cistern. I am rather impressed with my ability to manage what was needed. I have never been handy in the engineering department. I always call a plumber. But now I have a newfound confidence in my ability in the plumbing domain."

"OMG, Vivi! What happened to *Gullible You*? You are turning out to be much more relentless, premeditative, and gutsy than me. I am proud of you, girl! Forward-thinking, no-bullshit talking, pre-empting while lying low. I am super impressed. I am not sure the money will survive, but this story would be worth it even if it ended up as papier-mâché blocking the cistern."

"There's no stopping us now," I said. "Let us analyse this Glam Camp. We are going to see and deliver the report."

"How do you feel about Bash, Viv?"

"In truth, I don't know. I really like the guy. He is funny. He makes me smile, and from time to time, I see a glimpse of a person that feels hidden or cemented over. I think there is someone in there. But maybe he is too far down. Not even a grave robber may be able to dig out the diamond that I am sure lies within him. From the sounds of things, Bash has always been the blue-eyed face of the dark trade. I firmly believe his dad used him for that. What are your thoughts, Maddie? You are sharp and astutely intuitive. Can you see the man behind the shield?"

"I am not sure. My feeling is not overwhelmingly affirmative, but I cannot disregard the possibility. I also trust Theo's judgement. If Bash is a categoric bastard, then Theo would not put up with him. He would ban him and oust him. You and I both know that Theo has the power to do so. As far as I can see, Bash was never put in a place where he could become his true self. In that, I believe you have a point. Astutely made, albeit in a rather exaggerated poetic form," she laughed.

Maddie continued, "I think he doesn't really know who he is. So, he holds on to the things and people he knows. They include fast car driving, money trading, grave robbing, relic stealing, risk-taking, superficial opportunities and quick fix thrills, and to his friends from way back when, like us.

Whereas Theo has a strong heart, a bright mind, a sense of self, and a belief that wrong can be righted. He stands firm. Bash, however, wavers. He does not have the roots that Theo has. The interesting thing is that Theo can see the good side of Bash, though he does not have him by his side to develop Bash's strong sides and make him believe in better.

Both will always be boys.

The critical difference between them is that Theo is on the right side of being a bad boy, and Bash is not. I think part of Theo's frustration is that he wants to pull Bash to the right side of wrong, but he hasn't been able to so far. Since he can't get a hold of Bash, he stops him from putting us in any danger. Yet here we are. Acting behind Theo's back. We need to consider our moves, Viv."

"I know you are right, Maddie. I, too, feel we are being disloyal as far as Theo is concerned. I never intended that to be the case, but I can see clearly that this is the reality. If you were to ask me what the best outcome could be, I would answer that Bash gets separated from the forces that keep dragging him down. He needs to gain confidence that doing good can mean doing well.

It is not what he was brought up on or that his belief system was completely contaminated. Deep down, I believe he is kind-hearted and very able. His conversation is always superficial because he is scared to give information away. He is never sincere because laughter stops him from being pulled into a serious discussion. Superficiality and humour serve him and save him. Yet, at the same time, they have led to Bash being two dimensional rather than a complete person.

I believe he has the DNA, and I expect he is a fantastic guy underneath all the dirt and deceit. With the proper oxygen, care, support, love, and attention, he would have grown up to be like the rest of us. Because that is what we are lucky enough to have received from our parents, growing up. However, Bash lacks the confidence and know-how as well as the environment to dare to be authentic. It is tragic. He may be described as *damaged goods*."

"Viv, you have portrayed Bash to me in a new light. I clearly see that you may care for him more deeply than you realise yourself. We initially set off on a mission to set up Bash for failure and catch him and his dirty friends out. I think Zack and Nick are beyond hope, and frankly speaking, they are not our concern.

But we should and do care about Bash.

I think our mission is to get Bash to find a way to become the person he should have had the chance to become. He now has all the wealth he could ever want. If he never worked another day, he could live forever without a financial worry in the world.

We will have to mull this situation over. Let's go and check out the camp and get on with this paid job of ours and then consider our next moves."

Two hours later, we were off to the heliport. A cream coloured Bentley picked us up to take us there.

Glam Camp

On arrival at the heliport, we were greeted by a good look-ing guy in his forties. He introduced himself as Jordi. He was wearing an expensive-looking casual outfit. On his feet, he wore designer moccasins, and his tanned legs disappeared into a pair of fancy Bermudas. A beautiful belt and a simple white designer T-shirt completed the look.

He lifted his shades when he met us and greeted us with a peck on the cheek. "Welcome to Ronda, ladies. Let me drop you off at the camp. My brother Zack asked me to pick you up, and it is my pleasure."

Maddie shot me a look. *'Brother',* she mimicked while raising her eyebrows.

"Let me take those bags from you. Jump in the back. We aren't far away."

We had settled into the car. Maddie took out a notepad as well as her pen with the pink plaster.

She scribbled something on the pad and tilted it towards me. I read, *'Seems the guy driving is part of the Bermuda Triangle. Shorts and all.'* I tried not to laugh, and at the same time, I felt she was signalling to me to step up our act.

Maddie took the lead in making polite conversation. I didn't know how she managed to include the word *Berliner,* but I recognised the code. I sealed my lips closed and kept *schtum* just as we'd agreed.

Driving through the Ronda region was spectacular. The whitewashed houses looked petrified as they clung to the rock-face in their best attempt to stay safe and avoid freefalling into the dramatic ravine below.

When we arrived at the camp, around sunset, a man took our bags.

Jordi asked him to wait and said, "Ladies, you will meet the camp owner later. He was due to pick you up, but he was waylaid coming over from Morocco earlier in the day. That was the reason why I picked you up. He is now on his way and will be here within the hour. In the meantime, you will have time to relax and have some snacks. My apologies, but I need to go down to Gib to meet with someone at *The Rock Hotel.* I hope you have a good stay. Farewell, ladies." He jumped back into the car and sped off.

"The Rock Hotel," I said. "Now there is a trigger on memory lane for me. That was where Annie and I made our way onto the warship commanded by Captain James; he was a person we could have done with to stand by our side. With his MI5 security services hat on, he would have kicked Zack and Co into shape. But that is another story."

After Jordi went towards his car, the man carrying our luggage escorted us to a couple of adjoining tents. A heavily adorned purple velvet curtain between the tented quarters could be closed for privacy.

It looked as if we had just landed on our magic carpet and had been transported into an Arabian fairy tale.

Lanterns were lit as twilight descended. The nameless man placed our luggage down, bowed his head and walked away backwards, still facing us, then turned and exited the tent. I did not know whether we should have tipped him. There was no host around. We were left to our own devices, it appeared.

"Mads, may I speak?" I whispered when the man who carried the luggage had left.

"It's OK, Viv but try and be careful what you say."

Maddie held her spy pen in her hand and raised it up in front of me as if to remind me that we could not be careful enough.

After her softly spoken words, Maddie turned up the volume of her voice and said, in a bright, professional tone, "Now we are here, let us start our work."

She then pointed at the various pieces of furniture in the room using her pen as an indicator. I realised soon enough that she was filming the scene. It prompted me to take the two phones that Bash had given us out of the bag. I surreptitiously put one in each cup of my bra. Without speaking and using my eyes, I turned around and gave Maddie *The Look,* which said, '*follow me*'.

Maddie looked a bit confused, so with a bit of jerk of my head, I signalled to her to follow me, which she did. When we got outside, it was almost dark, and the torches around the glamp-site, as I now realised it should be called, were lit.

"What is this all that about Viv?" she asked me.

"Best to talk outside, Mads. You never know. You told me so."

Maddie laughed, "You are right, Bussi, but let's not go too

crazy, or they will think that we have escaped from some lunatic asylum. We have to be alert and, at the same time, we must appear professional and charismatic."

"You were waving your pen around like that back there. I thought you were on to something that I hadn't seen. And that Jordi guy. He says he is Zack's brother. But it seems he is a brother from another mother. I could not see any similarity, could you, Mads? Apart from the fact that they are both handsome, *Mudda Fukkas,* as Hélène would say. Though I miss her, it is good she isn't involved in this escapade, as by now, she would have been teasing the hell out of that Jordi guy. And as for Zack, she would have spat him out by now, maybe after she had her fun with him. If she weren't a woman, Hélène would be our *Super Stud.*"

"Viv, what were you doing back in the room before we came out? You were trying to hide something, but not terribly well. What did you pop under your sweater?"

"You mean you noticed?" I was taken aback. "Hmm, that is disappointing. I thought I managed to foil you, but then again, you are *über* astute. "

"May I remind you, *darling doughnut*, that I am not the one you are trying to keep secrets from. You are my partner in crime. Don't get carried away, or you may blow our cover."

"You are right, Mads. Will chill. In the meantime, let me give you your communication tool."

Maddie looked bemused. "What the hell is wrong with you, Viv? It seems you can't snap out of your new role."

As we spoke, a security light came on behind us. Or perhaps it was simply a floodlight on a timer, I was not sure. Maddie pulled out her pen and pointed it at me.

"Why are you filming me?" I asked her.

"Because you, you *Big Bloody Berliner,* are so hilarious, I will want this footage forever. When we are old, and you finally gain some wisdom, I can remind you of your foolish days."

"That is all well and good, but before you drop your guard, let me give you this before the owner chap comes around the mountain."

"What the hell, Buss. Have you lost the plot?"

"On the contrary. I am thinking ahead."

With that, I put both hands under my sweater. I fumbled around in my bra, which became undone in the process. I had imagined myself as an undercover cop, pulling the concealed weapons from their harness, in this case, the iPhones from my underwear. Instead, my detached bra caused the wedged phones to drop and slide down my tummy and onto the ground. The devices landed unceremoniously in front of my feet.

"You utter numpty, Viv!" Maddie collapsed, laughing. "Just stick to being your normal self and forget about anything else."

"Bloody bra. Always comes undone when you least need it to," I complained as I pulled up my shirt.

With my boobs out and my little Mayan man dangling between them, I leaned forward to reposition my breasts into my bra cups. It is a method I learnt when I went for my first luxury bra fitting.

I had always found it quite bizarre that women, usually older ladies, took your measurements as you stood in front of them with your twin peaks exposed. They solemnly measured you up, initially by putting the tape underneath your boobs onto your ribcage. After that, they moved the tape up to travel over your nipples and around your back. That apparently resulted in determining your correct cup size. I recalled the bizarre scenario at the Her Majesty's Bra Supplier, Rigby & Peller. With my torso still exposed, I told Maddie how I remembered the guy in full uniform who looked like a band leader minus his oversized drum. His job was to stand outside *Riggers & Pellers*, as we called the place in day to day lingo back in the day when I lived in London. He opened and closed the doors as women and girls came for their bra-fittings and purchased the finest of underwear.

The only thing he ever said was, 'Good Morning Madam', or 'Good Afternoon'.

"How can that be a job for any self-respecting bloke?" I asked. "I think I'd rather walk dogs in Hyde Park than open doors for women who are having their boobs measured by old biddies."

Maddie was laughing and attempting to film me.

"You can't laugh and film," I said. "The footage will be jerky."

I scooped my puppies up and put them back in their optimal cup position and did up my bra. I picked up the phones from the floor. As I stood upright, I looked up to see a guy standing behind Maddie.

I didn't know how long he had been watching us for, but he came forward and said, "Good evening, ladies. Forgive me for being late. I hope I am not disturbing anything?"

"Not at all," I answered as I put the phones into my pockets.

Maddie turned around to see whom I was speaking to and stopped dead in her tracks. "Bing!"

"Maddie! What in God's name are you doing here?"

I looked from one to the other, utterly confused. Then Maddie flashed him a most enchanting smile.

He walked towards her and embraced her. "Mad Maddie, my fair maiden. Where have you been hiding? Come on in. We need a drink, ladies. That's for sure."

Bing

"I hear you have been sent by *The Sharks*," Bing began. "I know that may sound like a weird opening line, but I can tell you this is not a game you want to play."

"What game Bing? What do you mean?"

"Maddie, we have some catching up to do. It has been over a quarter of a century since we last saw each other. At that time, you and I were *intense,* shall we say?"

"Was there something I missed, Mads?" I asked her.

"You mean, you didn't tell her about us?"

"I never told anyone about us," Maddie replied to Bing. "I promised I wouldn't and I never did."

"You are amazing, Mads. I always knew you were trustworthy. What happened to that guy, Theo, the one you stopped seeing me for?"

I was now utterly confused. But decided not to ask. This was the time to listen.

Maddie didn't say a word either, so Bing continued, "I received a message from Zack this morning. I was at my camp just outside Marrakech when he told me he needed me in

Ronda to meet two women who had been assigned the job of preparing a feasibility study. I assume he meant you two. I almost choked on my coffee when he effectively called it an assessment. I need to be able to trust you Maddie, in fact I must be able to trust you both implicitly. For your sakes. And mine. It is God's will and Zack's bad luck that we share history Maddie. I can give you some insight as to what is on going on here.

When we met at that trade fair in Geneva, Maddie, the one that happened every year, EIBTM I think it was called, I was working for upscale hotel chains. I got sick of it all. Political B.S. and a lot of nonsense about nothing of importance. I gave up my job and decided to travel the world. At one stage I was in Guatemala City when the volcano erupted. It had not done so for thirty years.

I recall receiving a Skype call from a friend of mine, Sebastian. He worked for a chain that was owned by an *über* rich guy. They had the Russian oligarchs, models and politicians staying with them, but they were getting fed up with being accommodated in the typical lap of luxury. They started wanting other things. Seb called me as he remembered that I was the guy who left the hospitality industry to explore new places and concepts. When he called me on Skype I answered him, wearing a mask to avoid inhaling the volcanic dust. I was staying in the Guatemala City and should have been on my way to the airport to fly to El Salvador. However, due to the volcano erupting, all flights were cancelled. The particles can bring down planes when they get into the engine."

"I know," I said. "I lost my friend that way in Costa Rica. She was scared to fly during the change of the millennium as she thought the computers would fail the flight systems. But then the volcano erupted, and the particles got into the engine, causing her plane to crash."

"Sorry to hear that," Bing said. "Latin America is a harsh continent. Mother Nature is in charge, no matter what people think they can control. But that is another story. To cut the saga short I was running out of money to fund my travels. Sebastian told me the owning company wanted to set up a luxury desert camp for *The Rich and Wealthy*. To provide them with far out experiences, for which they could charge the earth, simply since the offering was different. Sebastian recommended me to the owner because of my background in luxury hospitality and my sense of adventure. That was the space where you and I fused Maddie. The sweet spot between indulgence and thrill, always coupled with authenticity."

Bing looked at Maddie, "I thought you and I would always be together, eventually. But I am a fool. I waited too long and played the *Let's See* card."

"Yes, you are right," Maddie picked up where Bing left off. "And when you made steps towards moving forward, I played the *Cannot Commit Now* card. I think we didn't dare to be honest with ourselves. We made excuses."

"When I was ready, you weren't yet," Bing said.

"I wish someone had rattled my cage on time!"

"You never had a cage, Maddie. There was nothing to rattle. This was part of the overwhelming attraction I felt for you. A feeling that never left me. Bizarre to see you now, in such unexpected circumstances. All this has made me forget my manners.

I can't believe I have not offered you food and drink. What a swine I am. I am telling you I am being scouted to run the highest, most lavish, and luxurious glam camp in the desert, and you do not even have a glass of Champagne in your hand. Mea culpa!"

Bing pressed a concealed button next to where we were sitting and continued, "Anyway, I spoke to the owner, an Arab guy. He was very well connected and told me that if I was discreet and could offer the right level of service, the job was mine. I told this guy that I left hospitality employment to travel the world and then to open my own establishment to run as I saw fit. I told him I had no interest in being employed. I think this intrigued him. He said that he would invest in the camp and give me co-ownership. He would put in the funds and I was expected to put in the work. More importantly, I was told that discretion was always required. If there was a breach of secrecy, I would pay for it. If I accepted that as the only key condition, all I had to say was '*yes*' and fly to Morocco to get going with the camp on land that they'd already secured.

I was stuck in Guatemala City which was a dangerous place at the time. I couldn't go outside on account of the volcano and I was hotel bound. It gave me some time to think. I did not have any family commitments and, at the same time, I'd spent all my savings. It was time to replenish my funds.

In the spirit of loving both luxury and adventure, and with the promise of owning a business without having to put funds in, I accepted the offer. As soon as it was safe to do so, I flew to see the owners. They had a set up in Marbella, and somewhere in the Middle East but I never went there. We agreed my fee and they had a local lawyer draft a contract of co-ownership of the Glam Camp and the clause of secrecy. Little did I know that the secrecy clause did not only pertain to guest confidentiality but was embedded in subliminal reference to their illegal trade. In art, coffee, antiquities, and relics.

Well, I am not sure about coffee but that was the premise, perhaps for the coffee scent to disguise any shipments of the white powder. I did not find out straightaway, of course. We set up the camp, with the ultra-luxury equipment and arrangements. I was paid mega bucks. Naturally we had some teething problems and we sorted them out.

I'd learnt how to run a seven star hotel when I worked in the UAE, so I applied the same principles of service, experiences, and environment to the luxury camp. I stashed my cash and replenished my finances. I had been scraping the barrel and now the money was flooding in. I worked all hours of the day. Nobody asked questions. The owners let me get on with it. I only ever met the Owner Representative who you have met. His name is Zack. He calls himself the owner, but he isn't. He is the handsome face of the owner and he is supported by a guy who goes by the name of Jordi who says he is from Barcelona. I highly doubt that either of them is telling the truth. Then there is another chap who is probably harmless and does as he is told. That is Nick."

"Yes, we met Nick and Zack yesterday. Zack is clearly the one in charge," Maddie told Bing.

"He is, on the face of it," Bing continued, "but there is also a blond Arab guy. He is around our age. He is the son of the big owner whom I have never met. His name is Amin Bashir. He seems like a nice guy, though you wouldn't touch him with a bargepole because by default he is part of the *Dirty Boy Network*."

I shot a look at Maddie.

Bing silenced his words when the food arrived.

"If you don't mind, I think it is warmer to stay inside. When I press this button, Chef knows I want a selection of tapas and drinks. Whenever you are ready let me know and I push the same button twice and the heavier fare arrives. It's a discreet system that does away with intrusive order taking, and people trespassing and eavesdropping on conversations that should not be overheard. That is the type of clients and visitors we have here. The camp's name is simply '*Al Trab*', meaning *The Sand* in Arabic. It is the perfect name as in the end, the sole real purpose for this Royal Refuge is to cover up the traces of illegal trade. Over time I have learnt that clandestine activities are being conducted in my name, albeit partly, and on my watch.

One of the Berber guys, Sultan, my trusted camp director, smelled a rat early on. He knows the ways of the tribes and can interpret the vibes of the proverbial *Tam-Tam*. Through his connections and knowledge, we became increasingly aware of Arabic and African art making its way up to North Africa. The goods were then shipped on to Southern Spain, to make their way up to the international trading hubs of London and Geneva. Some pieces remained in Marbella. Nick who you met, was, as far as I can make out, a decent, though messed up, guy. He knows how to sail and he has travelled a fair amount. He spent some time in the Middle East and fought during Desert Storm. I once chatted to him over a bottle of whiskey. He told me that he was quite happy sailing a lovely yacht in the Med to take upscale guests on well-paid outings. He would do anything he once told me to get away from the recurring nightmares of the devastating war he had experienced.

Nick told me about older ladies on the yacht who slipped

him a few hundred dollars to make their orgasmic waves topple over on to their proverbial beaches. Seeing to the sexual demands of paying guests stopped Nick from being alone. He felt comforted in the presence of others. He was most vulnerable when he was alone with his thoughts. He told me that when he was not with anyone, he could easily be pulled back into reliving the hard and horrible conditions and events in the context of war.

After the second bottle of booze, Nick told me that he could still feel the shuddering air from under the helicopters as the blades cut the invisible atmosphere above him. He was not able to silence the constant ring of gunfire in his ear and the smell of old blood in his nose, as his comrades lying there bleeding. He could do absolutely nothing to stop these flashbacks and recurring nightmares. Nick said that there was an ever present taste of bitterness on his tongue as he could not escape the unpalatable memory of his horrific past. The petrified state of his shredded heart was tight and tortured. He lived both in fear and sorrow, having lost his friends who had fallen in that war zone."

Bing continued, "I have warmed to Nick. But he too, is playing a dangerous game, picking up illegal loads from Tangiers by yacht and dropping them off in Tarifa or sometimes Marbella, depending on the cargo.

"More wine?"

We both nodded and Bing refilled our glasses.

Bing then asked us, with an ironic smile, "Am I keeping you from your feasibility study?"

Maddie and I didn't laugh.

He got up. "Excuse me, ladies, I will be right back."

I looked at Maddie. "I didn't know what to say. Do you believe him, Maddie?"

"Without a shadow of a doubt Viv. He is a clean guy; caught in the biggest pile of poo you could shake a stick at."

"Clearly, there is no feasibility study needed and Zack can take the cash from the cistern and shove it up his bottom, but what is our next move? Where does that put Bash in this whole picture? When Bing mentioned this guy, Amin Bashir, the son of the head honcho in the Middle East, I knew he meant Bash. Can you believe I never thought about his first or last name until I saw his full name at the Reunion registrations? Even in our yearbooks, I remember it would always simply say '*Bash*' under his picture. How would Bing know Bash's full name? Or do you think Bash volunteered it?"

"I am not yet entirely sure, Viv. I am going to have to think various scenarios through. I am clear that Bing was telling the truth in broad lines. Zack is involved and powerful, but not the mastermind or big money behind this. That is Bash's dad. Unfortunately. Nick is trying to get away from his war trauma and make a buck on the side and Jordi is probably the logistics guy, moving goods, planning schedules, and meeting illegal trade contacts in charge of the *Black Ops Department*."

Bing came back in. "Sorry," he said. "Nature called, and nature is not the only one who did."

"What do you mean?" I asked.

"When I was in the bathroom, I received a call from Zack asking me how you are getting on."

"Bloody hell," Maddie said. "What did you tell him?"

"I told him that I don't know why you ladies are here and what his plan is. Zack told me that you being here is just a façade. That he needed you off his turf in Marbella and he needed to get Bash back on track."

Now Maddie and I were both thoroughly confused.

"Zack is not the brightest button in the box," Bing went on to say. "He is half British and half Spanish. From experience I know how to push his emotional buttons. I just must frustrate him and I can trigger a response. He told me that he was angry with Bash. I asked him why. Zack said that he had agreed for you two to come down as Bash had alluded to contacts you had as it related to art. You in Africa, Maddie, and Vivi, in the Middle East and even Central America. He mentioned some Jade Man, but that's where he lost me. It turns out that Bash pulled back on wanting to pursue the available network. It seems he was wobbling and becoming susceptible to one or both of you. I don't know."

He took a sip of his drink. We both remained silent.

"It seems Bash has changed since he went to Switzerland recently. Zack has no idea what is going on. Bash has always been a useful and easy card to play. He has roguish looks but he is blue eyed and from that messed up perspective, can gain trust in a brown-eyed Arab world. It is ridiculous but there is some truth in it as I have found out first-hand."

He looked at Maddie, "If you and I had ever got together, we would've mixed your deep brown eyes with my light blue ones, then we could have created the perfect jade eyed next generation to drive the trade, just like Bashir Senior has done with Bash all his life."

"Bing. This is one hell of a story but we have limited time. What trouble are you in?" Maddie asked him directly.

"Interpol has been alerted to the trade at *Al Trab*. Because of that, Zack moved me to Ronda. You were sent here as some sort of an alibi, though I have not quite worked that one out. Bash is clearly not in favour with his father or with Zack at the moment. Bash's dad will never come to Marbella as he would immediately be picked up by international intelligence, but Bash should really get the hell out of Spain too before things totally go tits up."

"What about you, Bing? Where does that leave you?" Maddie asked.

"I don't know," he replied. "Fighting the Arabian Mafia is not something I have done before. I am so sorry you have inadvertently landed in this big pile of poo. We need to figure out what to do. On the upside, I must tell you how amazed and grateful I am that we have crossed paths again, Maddie. They may be smugglers' paths but the storm cloud has a silver lining. Whatever happens I know you are well, alive, and still that wonderful woman I fell in love with all those years ago."

Maddie was silent. Tears filled her eyes. She shook her head and squeezed her eyes shut, as if to shake off a feeling too painful to feel again.

She pulled herself together.

"Let's think our way out of this," Maddie said. "Let it all go for tonight and we will meet for breakfast in the morning."

Bing stood up and then bent down and kissed Maddie on the top of her head and stroked her hair.

He looked at me and said, "I am happy to meet you, though I wish it was in more pleasant circumstances."

Theo

"**M**addie, we need to ask Theo to step in. There is no one else who we can turn to. Even though he is clean, Theo knows how to play dirty. His father was in the illegal trade and he has seen it up close and personal. We need to own up and ask him what to do."

Maddie thought about it. "You are right Viv. As far as I can see, there are two people who are bearing the brunt of this: Bash and Bing. I know we won't come out of it smelling of roses, as we've deceived Theo, even though there was no intent of that.

We need to keep a clear head. The only person who can really help us out and whom we trust is Theo. He may be furious with us and he has reason to be. But we must be brave. We must tell him. There is nothing else for it. He may tell us to sort out our own sorry saga, but we must call. It is six or seven hours earlier in San Jose than here. We need to act now, before bedtime in Central America."

I felt sick as I sent Theo a message via WhatsApp: *'Theo, we are in trouble. With we, I mean Maddie, myself, and Bash. Please can we call you. Maddie and I are sorry, but we don't know what else to do. I think we are in a dangerous situation. And Bash is, too. We are sorry. Please help.'*

Within minutes, Theo responded: '*What is going on, Sis? You got me worried. I am on my way to Amilcar's House. He is not well. I need to make it up the drive to La Hacienda. When I get there, I will call you. Skype?'*

I respond: '*Yes please, Skype.'*

The minutes passed by painfully slowly. Twenty two minutes later the Skype call came though from Costa Rica. I felt a pit in my stomach as I answered the call. I thought talking without video would be easier so I chose that option. It took a while to connect.

"Put your video on," Theo instructed. There is no gentle introduction or asking after us. "Tell me, what is going on." His video was on and he had Amilcar next to him, who looked awful though managed to raise his gentle smile.

"Bash is in trouble and Maddie's friend, Bing. I have a feeling that probably we are, too."

"Where are you?"

"Outside Ronda, in Southern Spain."

"Send me your location by WhatsApp, before you continue."

I did as Theo had asked.

"Now, tell us what is going on. Be clear and concise. I want facts. Not emotions."

Maddie and I managed to tell Theo the story of how we had accepted Bash's invitation to go to Marbella. We told him we wanted to set up a business and look at ways to create multiple income streams.

"Never mind about all that. Cut to the chase."

Maddie took the lead and talked Theo and Amilcar through

the events. Amilcar did not speak, though he was clearly listening attentively. Theo asked questions. We answered.

Then Theo asked, "Who is this Bing guy?"

I looked at Maddie. What to say?

I respect Maddie until this day as she told Theo, "He is the guy I met after school and before you and I met up again."

"You never told me about him," Theo said, sounding as cold as stone.

"Maybe I should have," Maddie responded, "but it was clear that Bing and I were never going to be together so I did not think there was any point in telling you about him."

Theo flinched. Amilcar put a soothing hand on Theo's arm. Theo breathed in and held his breath. Then he closed his eyes and exhaled. Regaining his composure, he asked questions, probing deeper. I thought he was amazingly clever at putting the picture together. He recapped his understanding. All the while Amilcar was listening but never said a word.

"In short," Theo said, "You and Vivi are being used as a decoy for Zack who is the guy on the ground for Bash's dad, to get rid of this Bing guy, because he is not OK with illegal trade happening at the Camp, which this Bing chap partially owns. Bash appears to be rather useless in the whole thing, but he is the one who introduced you to Zack. Then dirty boy Zack saw the opportunity to get you two girls to meet Bing and pretend it was a clean business and a paid-for feasibility study of the camps. No doubt the next step will be to implicate Bing and get rid of him so that clandestine trade can continue and not be jeopardised by some high luxury camp operator and goody two shoes, jeopardising their illegal trade. The Bashir Emporium will not let that happen. They chose the camp in the middle of the desert to run their business from and to do their deals there. They will never let a small fry guy put a spanner in their wheels. Because that is what Bing is to them. A little fly in their lucrative ointment. It's obvious."

"Wow," I said, in awe. "I did not see that picture. Do you think that is how it is, Theo? How do you think Bash fits in? And what is the Bashir Emporium?"

"Viv, let Maddie and me handle this. She is used to knob heads. The Bashir Emporium is the underground network that Bash's father runs. The Big Bashir. Bash is just a gofer. Albeit a wealthy one. But let's not get into Bash. He will fit in with whatever Amilcar and I decide. Though he needs a reminder about who is in charge. He was badly behaved on the Mountain and needs to remember who the boss is. Listen very carefully. We need to isolate Zack. We cannot get to Bash's dad yet, the Big Bashir."

At that point Theo looked at Amilcar, who gave him a hardly discernible nod.

Theo continued, "Bash needs to be extracted before the proverbial poo hits the fan. Get him out of Marbella, out of the hotel and, most importantly, away from Zack. Zack is a bully whose ego is inflated and it's about to cause Bash's extinction. Before Zack feels cornered, Bash needs to be taken out. Maddie, call me on Skype in ten minutes. Vivi, wait for instructions from Maddie or me. Do not take orders from anyone else. Is that all clear?"

We both nodded. With that, Theo hung up.

"Bloody hell, Mads. This is bad. Talking of which, do you see how terrible dear Amilcar looked?"

At that moment the phone that Bash had given me, rang.

"Answer it, Viv," Maddie says. "Keep your cool."

"Hello," I answered and put the call on speaker phone.

"Hello, it is Jordi here. How are you ladies doing? How is your study going? I finished my business at *The Rock* and wondered whether you wanted any company?"

"Thank you, Jordi, for checking up on us. Hope your meeting in Gibraltar went well. Thank you, but both of us turned in early. We completed the first site inspection and I must say, you have a great camp here. We are due to continue our work at the crack of dawn." I tried to forget what Malcolm the DJ had said about Dawn's crack during the Reunion, just before I had to deliver my speech.

"OK, fair enough. Let me put you on to Bash. He is right next to me."

Oh no! I reeled.

Maddie kept her cool and looked me in the eye, as if to say, 'You can do this'.

"Hey Vivikins, how are you?" Bash asked.

"We are great, Bash. This camp is awesome though both Maddie and I have noticed some cracks in the management that need attention. But all in all, we have a good impression. Tomorrow we will dig a little deeper."

"I wouldn't mind digging a little deeper with you," Bash whispered. "Why am I on speaker, Viv?"

I looked at Maddie who closed her eyes and nodded encouragingly.

"I can tell you, as long as you are not on speaker," I said, in a provocative voice.

"You are in my ear. Though I wish you were in my arms," Bash replied, in a low voice.

"Are you far from here?" I asked him.

"Not a million miles away. Jordi and I wanted to pass by. I was with him in Gib, a last minute meeting, but he says you are not up for it."

"Bash, can you give me a minute and call me back in five?"

"Is everything alright, Viv?"

"All is good but I need the loo. One of those un-negotiable situations."

"Sure thing. Will call back in five or seven. Take your time."

"Good job, Viv," Maddie said, as I hung up.

"We need to call Theo and Amilcar. Maybe they will know how to handle this."

We redialled the Skype number. Within two rings Theo answered. Amilcar was no longer on the call.

"Where is Amilcar?" I asked.

"He is resting now."

I updated Theo that Bash had called and would call me back shortly.

"Ask him if you can meet tomorrow. That way you can respect the work that needs to be done. Tell him that though you are tempted to spend the night with him, it would not be professional to create diversions, tempting though they may be. Or create any excuse for him not to come tonight. Use your imagination. By tomorrow night, Spanish time, lunchtime Tico time, I will have a better idea of what is needed."

Theo looked directly at Maddie, "I must speak to this Bing guy. But before that, I must speak to you, Maddie. In private. I need info on this guy and you are clearly in a good position to give that to me." Theo was making a point. He clearly did not like the fact that Maddie had been in a relationship with

Bing all those years ago.

"Call Bash, Viv and Maddie, stay on the line with me."

I called Bash. "I don't know what to say, Bash. I am not sure whether it was the calamari earlier or what, but I have just thrown up every tapa I stuffed into my greedy mouth earlier. Maddie is getting me a bucket. I am sure I will feel better soon. I didn't feel great earlier, but I so wanted to hear your voice and see you. But this is not good. Seems like I ate something between the hotel and the camp that did not agree with me."

"I am so sorry to hear that Viv, how nasty. Did it happen within the confines of the hotel or the camp? If so, I will fire the executive chef immediately."

"No," I said, followed by, "give me a sec, please."

I made it sound like I was being sick and then I said, "Thanks Maddie darling, that was just in time. Can you pass me the towel and maybe a glass of water?"

I then picked up the phone again and said, "Really sorry, Bash, this is not ideal."

"Vivi, I am so sorry. Take some rest. Drink plenty of water and if you are not OK in the morning, screw the feasibility study. I am going to go back to Marbella and I'll send in the food inspectors. If your food poisoning started here, or at the Camp, heads will roll. I will call you in the morning. Take care and rest up."

I felt wretched.

Trading Places

Maddie finished her call with Theo. He instructed her to ask Bing to connect with him on a Skype. Maddie left Bing to talk to Theo and surreptitiously *forgot* her pen in Bing's quarters.

When Maddie returned to where I was, I said, "I guess we have to trust in Theo. We always do. After this episode he may no longer think of us being his untouchables. More likely, we will be his *screw-upables*."

"Let's try and get some sleep, Viv. We are in deep dung. But at least we are in it together."

"Thank God for Theo. Even his name means *Divine Gift.*"

"He is divine," Maddie said. "The way he takes control. He is a powerful force. You can rely on him and that cannot be said for some, like my ex Manu. Though let us make no mistake, we owe Theo, Viv. Nobody in life gives you something for nothing. Unless it is the smile of your children and even that changes after the age of four."

"Easy on, Mads. That's a bit dark. I don't think Theo is that way. Remember he gave me my little jade man all these years ago? That was from the goodness of his heart. And to celebrate our friendship. He said he hoped I would be his *Forever Sister*."

"You know how I feel about Theo, Viv. But I have seen more lies and intrigue than you can shake a stick at. I am wired differently to you and have first-hand experience of matters I have not yet shared with you. I am tarnished perhaps by the brush of deceit and have seen some things that would make your head spin. Illegal trade, drugs, you name it. It was all par for the course in Africa. I love that you see the good in people. Before you tell me, Theo is amazing, I agree. But there is more to *Angel Face* than meets the eye. On that note, let's close ours and get some rest."

Maddie blew me a kiss goodnight and went into her bedroom, adjacent to mine.

After she switched her bedside light off, the tent went dark. I must have slept pretty much immediately, but woke up during the night, then I tossed and turned for a few hours. Finally, I fell into a deep sleep.

When I woke up, I looked at my phone to check the time. It was just past nine o'clock. I noticed a missed call from Bash. I lay on my bed, thinking about the events of the night before. Meeting Bing, my lying to Bash about being sick, involving Theo whom I had not been straight with. It all felt very ugly. I jumped under the shower to try to wash off the sense of feeling dirty somehow. I wet my hair but I did quickly, as I assumed the water supply in the camp may be limited.

Better not get caught with my hair fully shampooed and then not have the water to rinse it out.

Dressed in a freshly laundered, waffle cotton bathrobe, with a towel wrapped around my hair like a turban, I went to see how Maddie was. I peeked behind the heavy purple curtain that divided our quarters; It was left open last night but had been unhooked and draped across the doorway.

Very appropriate, I thought.

The dramatic curtain had fallen signifying *The End of Act One.*

How many acts would there be, I wondered, with a shudder.

I couldn't see Maddie and noticed her belongings were stacked on the colourful Arabesque patterned bedcover. It seemed as if her bed had not been slept in. *Oh, my Lord. Surely not?*

Did Maddie spend the night with Bing after she switched off the light? Had she been planning it all along?

Get a grip, you sad moo. No need to start wondering about Maddie's motives, too.

I snapped out of my swirling thoughts and slipped into my clothes. Feeling chilly, I took one of the warm sweaters Bash had delivered to our rooms before we travelled to Ronda. It was a gorgeous soft Merino wool top in a pale pink blush. I pulled it over my head and slipped my arms into it. It felt snug and it made me feel even worse about lying to Bash. Blush was perhaps the appropriate colour. I should be ashamed of my behaviour. He was a rogue perhaps, but he was caring and attentive too. I felt a warmth for him and smiled. I hoped he would forgive me. In time, I was sure all would be clear as day as to what was happening here and we would all carry on as usual.

I left the tented accommodation to find Maddie and Bing sitting in what looked like the *Living Room*. Although the shape of the tent was a Berber design, it was cream coloured rather than brown. Along the seams, it has the same Henna Tattoo patterns that I'd noticed and loved when we had our *hot chocolate experience* at *Ventana Romana*. There was a link in the repetition of the pattern on various items and in multiple places.

I started to think perhaps I had a penchant for seeing connections.

I was aware that I saw correlations and synergies in situations that combined to form new and positive outcomes. In this case, I saw a link, though my mind had no idea how to connect it in context to the situation we were in. What was the story? What predicament were we in?

"Good morning," I said as I walked in and greeted Maddie and Bing.

They both looked up. There were papers everywhere. Maddie had her laptop open. There was an ashtray full of cigarette butts, as well as Maddie's wounded pen with its bright pink plaster lying on the table.

"Hi Viv," Maddie said.

"Good morning. Fancy a coffee?" Bing asked me. "I will bring a fresh pot and get some breakfast too, if you ladies are ready for a bite?"

"Very ready," Maddie smiled. It seems like she hadn't slept.

Was I right, had Bing and Maddie spent the night together? I felt like an intruder. *On reflection they were not behaving like love birds or sex infused people who reconnected after a quarter of a century and had simply picked up where they left off.*

"Viv?" Maddie asked. "Where is your head at? Are you ready for breakfast?"

"Oh, sorry. Yes, that would be lovely. My apologies, I am a bit vague this morning. How are you feeling?"

"Actually, we were up all night, Maddie and I," Bing said.

See, I was right. I thought that Maddie liked Theo and now that she'd met Bing again, she went straight back to him.

"Viv. Snap out of it." Maddie said. "Nothing is going on between us. We have bigger fish to fry and to figure out, so stay with the programme, *Berliner Bärchen.*"

I felt relieved somehow to be on equal footing and not like the third wheel.

Nothing was going on between them.

"I am going to debrief you on last night," Maddie said. "And, before you ask, yes I smoked my head off. I puff like a locomotive when I need to plot a plan. Bing told me about his conversation with Theo. Bing explained that the Glamp Site in Morocco is co-owned by him, but that Bash's dad is a hardcore underworld boss who strategically used the logistically advantageous location for illegal trade place, also dubbed *Trading Places* by those in the know. Bing explained to Theo that he signed a secrecy act and that he is now being threatened by Zack and his men to keep quiet about what he knows, or else he will be silenced in other ways.

Zack told Bing to come to Ronda to meet with official feasibility experts. That is where you and I come in, as industry professionals. It is on record that we have flown in. We are registered at the hotel and that we have taken a helicopter flight to the Glam Camp. All our journey has been recorded on CCTV. There are plenty of witnesses, genuine or bribed, should they be needed. Paying us a small sum under the premise of doing a feasibility study for the owner is just a convenient opportunity to divert from the real matter in hand. Bing explained that he believed we are a simple decoy as Zack himself said. The main aim was to dispose of any barrier to business. In this case, that was Bing."

"You and Maddie are considered a timely opportunity to speed up being able to get rid of me," Bing reiterated.

"I thought you went to sleep when you switched the light off," I said to Maddie.

"I didn't want to disturb you, but I lay fully dressed on top of the covers trying to figure out what to do. Thinking in the dark allows me to focus. While lying on the bed, I realised that I had left my pen with Bing and thought it was worth picking it up and to see whether he was still awake."

"And I thought you were coming to see me," Bing laughed, "but all you were after was a pen that looked like it had been through the wars and then ended up in a kindergarten where the teacher popped a happy plaster on its wounds."

We both looked at Bing.

"You are talking rubbish, Bing. You are clearly less good at not sleeping for a night than I am. Why don't you take a nap and let me fill Viv in?"

"You may be right, Maddie. I don't think any amount of coffee will keep me awake. Excuse me. I should be as good as new in an hour or two." Bing sauntered off to crash into bed.

"Tell me your side of the story, Mads. It's good that Bing left. I want to understand."

"Here, have a ciggie. It helps to smoke."

"No thank you, Inspector Maddie. But you go ahead. I will stick to coffee and chocolate to get me through this."

I retrieved the box of chocolates Bash had given to us for our trip and settled in opposite Maddie, in the Henna Tattoo Tent. Maddie told me about her conversation with Theo.

"After Bing spoke to Theo last night, Theo called me again. He told me to meet up with Bing and find as much information about him and his business as I could and to debrief Theo afterwards. I felt a little disloyal to Bing but followed Theo's lead. Theo is the leader of the pack and knows what he is doing. He gave me instructions and told me to follow them. Theo said he meant no harm, but that he needed me to be the only contact, so that there would not be any misunderstandings that could be cause for a lack of clarity and therefore be a risk."

I had a feeling there were more details that may have been discussed, though I knew that Maddie was much better at these things and I was happy for her to take the lead with Theo, my Tico Brother.

"This is going to be rather different from what you might expect, Viv. Stay with me on the ride as I take you through Theo's instructions. Let's fill up our coffee mugs and I will spill the beans."

Mayan Jade Man

"I spoke to Theo last night, as you know. He said that he needs you with him at Amilcar's Hacienda. He says there is little time. I am sorry Viv, to have to tell you this. Amilcar is in his last days. He is very weak and asked to see you."

"Oh my God, poor Amilcar. He has been so sick for years. I have never known him any other way. I can't quite take in what you are telling me."

"I know Buss, it is beyond tough and very sad indeed. But he asked for you to go and see him."

"Of course, I will but what about you? I can't leave you in this mess. I can't just go off, no matter that I know I must."

"Don't worry Viv. Bing is here and Theo is on call. There is an issue that needs resolving and I will manage that. Your job is to see Amilcar before it's too late."

"If you are sure, you can manage whatever situation we are in, then yes I will go. Though I have no clue about arranging a flight to San José from here."

"Theo has made reservations for you. You take a flight out of Malaga airport and then to San José, via Madrid. Theo asked me to check with you, but in parallel he made your reservation. I guess he knew you would agree. We will travel to Malaga with Bing. You will go north. We will go south to the desert camp. Theo has a plan that he has not fully shared with me, but I trust him. He told Bash to meet us in Malaga and to come with Bing and me to Morocco."

I felt a twinge in my gut. If I was being honest, I kind of missed Bash, I would have been pleased if he were flying with me to Costa Rica. We could then really talk on the flight and I could get to know him better. Bash bore the brunt of Theo's sharp tongue and strong personality, but I couldn't see Bash as all bad. He made me laugh. Not that laughter alone would ever be enough. I knew that from experience. The fact of the matter was, Bash would be travelling south.

With a smile and a rush of blood to both my cheeks and puss, I remembered our time in the steam room in *La Résidence,* when Bash said he was going to explore my southern region. It had been fun and good. But no follow up to speak of. It was an unfinished story. I decided to go with the flow. Theo asked for me to come. As did Amilcar. There was no question. I was Costa Rica bound.

When we arrived in Malaga, I had hoped to see Bash, but I didn't as I had to catch my flight on time. I left a message with Maddie to give to him.

My note to Bash read; '*Sorry to miss you. It has been an odd time. If I don't see you anytime soon, the money is stuffed in the toilet in the suite. We don't want it. We never did the job. Talking of suite, you are so sweet with all the thoughtful items you packed for Maddie and me. Hope all is good. Look forward to meeting up in the desert some other time.*

Take care, V x'

I used to fly into San José at least once or twice a year. When I worked in hospitality, before moving into consulting, I literally flew three weeks out of four. It became too much, eventually. While I loved to travel, I just wanted the world to stop, so I could get off. On one trip I travelled from Egypt to Chicago and then on to Costa Rica with a stop somewhere that I can't recall. I was utterly exhausted. Moving from one airport on to a plane, to another airport and on to the next plane, can feel endless and depressing. Some journeys wear you down.

On arrival in Costa Rica, however, happiness greeted you.

Families were waiting for their loved ones. Holding oversized Disney toys, flowers, and gifts, with broad smiles on their faces and the sound of laughter and Latin music coming from their phones, or ghetto blasters. The beautiful Tica girls in their pretty mini dresses, with their mothers and grandmothers in Bermudas. Even in broad daylight they took any opportunity to salsa. Older men, well into their silver years, flaunted their stuff and moved as if age were of no concern, sliding their arms around the waists of their wives and *amores*.

I loved feeling the energy, the positivity, and their carefree ways.

They greeted each other with Pura Vida, Pure Life.

Arriving at Juan Santa Maria International Airport was in stark contrast to landing in Budapest during winter. At that time the airport was still called by its old name, *Ferihgy*. Having left the plane, I made my way to baggage reclaim. Around the slowly moving belt, people stood motionless like petrified pigeons forming an inanimate sea of grey. The black and brown coloured suitcases were gently vomited on to the rickety belt and chugged around until they were claimed, solemnly and without sound, by a person who looked the same as the next. Clad in dark grey coats, gloves, and hats, with only their solemn faces showing.

Hungarian music, though beautiful, was haunting and sad, born out of pain. And this was Hungary, post-Soviet rule. *Imagine how much worse it worse it would have been before the liberation?*

I could appreciate the beauty of Buda and Pest, but arriving at this most beautiful of cities, did not make me feel joyous on arrival.

As for Costa Rica. It made my heart sing, my blood speed up and my eyes shine, as if I have Prosecco running through my veins.

For me, Costa Rica was a very firm favourite place on God's planet and somewhere I felt alive and connected.

Theo had booked me a business class ticket. The sweetheart. The cabin was almost full, a well-dressed bum on each seat, except on the chair next to mine. I know I had plenty of space but nonetheless I relished the thought of a transatlantic flight with nobody sitting next to me. No one to be polite to.

I had had some nutters sitting next to me in my time. One person tried to convert me to an obscure faith I can't recall, and another fainted in the aisle when he was about to return to his seat from a bathroom stop. A doctor had to be called and, in the end, the pilot had to divert the plane to Iceland, where the passenger was offloaded. But he had forgotten his book on the tray next to me. It lay open.

When I closed the book to hand it to the stewardess, the title read in great big letters, 'Fear of Flying'.

I took the laundered blanket and pillow out of their plastic covers. I had not realised just how exhausted I was. I curled up and fell asleep. I woke up somewhere midway across the Atlantic and with my eyes still closed, I stretched out my arms. My right side was restricted on account of sitting in the window seat, but I extended my left arm far and wide, until it felt something unexpected. I opened my eyes and adjusted myself. There was someone sitting in *my other seat*. Still slightly comatose, I did a double take. There before my eyes was a seriously good looking guy. Clad in white and cream linen, he was smiling charmingly at me.

"Sorry to be in your stretching range. It seems you would prefer me at arm's length, or perhaps in another row altogether. I would have chosen another seat to let you sleep in peace and have your space, but the whole cabin was booked out."

Still not with it, I replied, "I wasn't expecting you there. Why are you late? Everyone had already boarded and the man in the fluorescent jacket had come in to close the flight. I used to work for an airline. I know when the flight is ready for departure. At that point, no other people can board. Unless they are a pilot or something or a prince or whatever. But you, you were not here then, when the man closed the flight. Are you a pilot or a prince? Who are you, that you could come on board after the flight was closed?"

"Can I order you a coffee? Or are you planning to go back to sleep? I must say you seemed to be busy the first few hours of the flight. I don't mean to eavesdrop but when you mumbled,

'*I stuffed it down the loo*', you had me intrigued."

"Oh my God! What else did I say?"

"Something about '*Bash*'. It sounded like the name of a ball-game though the smile on your face suggested something else. You were drooling a bit. I hope you don't mind, I just wiped it from your chin. I thought it best to leave the napkin there in case you slept all the way to San José and another trickle needed to be stopped in its tracks."

"You could have just woken me up, or do you go round clearing dribble from people's drooling mouths?"

"Not typically," he smiled. "It was a first for me. I apologise. You are right. I should have simply let you be."

"Yes, you should have. Now, can we drop the subject?"

"Of course."

"Thank you. And since the matter is now closed, I would like to say thank you, you know, for erm, cleaning me up."

"Sure thing, Ms...?"

"Vivika."

"Now that is a name that suits you. It is derived from the Spanish *Vida,* meaning *Life.*"

"And what name do you go by Mr Dribble Wiper?"

"My name is Wai."

"Why?"

"It is W-A-I. Yes, why not? In Spanish that translates into *Si Como No.*"

"Oh my God, that is my favourite hotel on God's planet," I said.

"Is it? Tell me what you like about it?"

"I just love that eco hotel on the Pacific. The owner is a brilliant eco warrior, a nature ambassador, and a visionary.

Only one tree was cut down when the hotel was built. The people who work there are great too. I have stayed there often. I love it!"

"That is really good to hear. Will you be staying there on this trip?" Wai asked.

"Why do you ask, Wai?" I teased.

"I can see you are going to have some fun with my name as we wing our way over the big blue. I know my name is a bit unusual. These Berliners were certainly confused when I went to do my recording."

I smiled to myself recalling Maddie's story about JF Kennedy calling himself *Ein Berliner*, a jelly doughnut. A common occurrence it seemed.

"Let me explain the context of where my name came from. Wai is an abbreviation of *Warner*. My parents who are pure Costa Ricans, or Ticos, were watching an American movie. In the credits it said, '*Warner Brothers*'. They liked the sound of it and called me '*Warner*'. A strange fact. I have a friend of my age who is called Usnavy."

"Usnavy?"

"You pronounce the *v* more like a *b*, but you write it U-S-N-A-V-Y. It shares similar inspirational roots with my name. But this time it refers to the 'US Navy'. My buddy's Spanish speaking Tico parents had no idea what 'US Navy' meant. They liked the ring of the words they read on the TV and called their son Usnavy, Navy for short, which in Tico Spanish sounds like *Usnabi*. We call him Nab."

"So, what would that make me, with the two *v*'s in my name?"

"Bibika. Bibi or Bika, for short. Cute, though I must say I

find Vivika enchanting. So, tell me, if you allow me to enquire, will you be staying at Si Como No during your stay?"

"I am not sure. I am not clear on my movements yet. My trip here is very unexpected. The place where I am going first is not too far inland from the Pacific. I am sad to say I have come to say goodbye to my good friend."

"I am sorry to hear that," Wai said.

"I know. Or rather I don't know, really. I am blessed he asked me to come and so sad at the thought to have to say goodbye. I don't know how I will be. This is not something you can practice. What will be, will be."

"*Que será, será.*"

"Let us change the subject. I have done spit and dribble, no need to add tears. Wiping those away will be messier as my lashes are covered in mascara."

"Would not want to see you cry, but if you need some tunes to meditate to or relax by, let me give you something."

Wai opened his bag which looked like nothing I had seen before.

"What an amazing pouch. What are all the moving parts. It looks almost knitted from leather covered metal linkages."

"You have an excellent eye, Bibika. They are metal ring pulls from cans. The waste is collected and covered in leather off-cuts and made into designer bags, accessories, curtains, and other fashion and interior design items. Let me tell you about that in a minute if you want to hear. But first, this is for you."

Wai put his hand inside the bag and retrieved a CD. He opened it, took a pen out of his pocket, and wrote a message on the inside of the cover that lined the Perspex case. Then, he gave it to me.

'Bibika, I have enjoyed our encounter in the sky. May these tunes soothe your soul. Vaya con Dios, siempre. May God be with you always, Wai xx'

"That is so kind of you. What is on the CD?"

"My music. I play the flute. I have just come back from a recording session with the Philharmonic Orchestra in Berlin. These babies are hot off the press. I hope you like it."

I turned the case round. On the front was a picture of Wai and the title of the album, *Sueños en el Cielo*. My throat closed as I thought, in pain, about Amilcar.

"I have upset you, Bika. I am sorry. Are you OK?"

"You were not to know, Wai. The place where I am going is called *La Hacienda Sueño en el Cielo*. Such a weird coincidence that your album is called that too."

"You are going to see Amilcar?" Wai asked.

"Do you know him?"

"Amilcar is the *Padre*. He is the man behind the *Loving Little Lids Foundation* which we founded together back in 2002. My bag is one of the LLLF creations. It is one of the earlier social enterprises. The business model uses for-profit mechanisms, to do good. Effectively it is a hybrid company, that sits somewhere between commercial enterprise and purpose driven initiatives that help people and the planet. I met Amilcar via my buddy, Usnavy, *Nab*, whom I just told you about. He is friends with Theo, who is Amilcar's protegé. I came back from Berlin to say goodbye to Amilcar too. We are both flying in for the same reason. I will be staying in Si Como No."

"Oh, my Lord."

I was flummoxed. I could not take it all in.

"I am confused. You said Theo is Amilcar's protegé. Surely

you mean the other way around. Theo is older and wiser; he is the driving force in that relationship. I have known both Amilcar and Theo for over thirty years, and Theo has always taken care of Amilcar. I have seen it before my eyes."

"Amilcar has always been sickly to the great disappointment of El Comandante, his father. He was a ferocious man with a black greedy heart. He was known for his illicit trade, grave robberies, and exquisite Pre-Colombian Art collections. Most of the artefacts he stashed in *La Hacienda*. The fact that the estate became a coffee plantation was simply a way to steer authorities away from putting a spotlight on the illegal trade. El Comandante positioned himself as a *Coffee Baron*, though he knew nothing about coffee. To make sure there were actual coffee producing activities going on, he took on a guy by the name of Curtis Coffee, who was always at the estate and became close with Amilcar. Almost like his resident caretaker and token substitute dad. El Comandante was hardly ever there.

Curtis ran the coffee business. El Comandante would send stolen goods to *La Hacienda* for safekeeping. But he was not often there. If anything needed shifting, then Theo took care of it.

Amilcar's dad had a particular penchant for Jade. Jade was incredibly important to the Mayans in the past. It is believed that it could take on great spiritual and religious significance. The stone's green colour lent it to associations with water and vegetation, and it is symbolically associated with life and death in the eyes of the Mayans. At the time of the Mayans, jade was more precious than gold.

This stone is reputed to bring beauty and long life to the wearer. It evokes wisdom, peace, harmony and devotion to one's higher purpose, and aids the person in finding their life path and manifesting their dreams into reality. Jade is worn to attract love or is given to another in the hope of obtaining love. Amilcar lived with so much jade around him, but never with any love from El Comandante. Amilcar was a great disappointment to his father. Not only was he weak physically, but nor was he flamboyant and loud like his dad, who always needed to be the centre of attention.

El Comandante was a bully and Amilcar, his victim, made from his own flesh and blood, though apparently without much of El Comandante's despicable DNA. Amilcar was intelligent and quiet. His dad hated him.

Amilcar's mother died years before, I don't know how. Eventually Amilcar was sent abroad to some place in the mountains in the Swiss Alps, as far as I heard. For fresh air, they said. El Comandante continued to trade and forged links with The Orient and Africa, as well as Europe. This was where Amilcar's dad met Theo's father. One thing that El Comandante never realised was that his son, Amilcar, may have been weak in body but he was highly intelligent and astute from a cerebral perspective.

Amilcar figured out his father's undercover actions and mapped his movements. One day, when Amilcar was away in Switzerland, his father went missing. He could not be found until years later when he was discovered in a Mayan cave. When grave robbers tried to raid the cave, thinking it was still virgin and full of treasure, what they found was the disintegrated body of the once feared and sadistic Comandante. A mere skeleton of a man who had rotted away in the cave that he himself had previously pillaged.

With the death of El Comandante, the illegal trade stopped. Amilcar changed the name of the estate to *La Hacienda Sueño en el Cielo* meaning *Dream in Heaven*, from what it was called by his father, *La Hacienda Sueño en el Suelo*, which meant *Dream on Earth*.

Amilcar said that his father raped the earth but that he could never hurt heaven, so he changed the name of his home after his dad went *'missing'*."

Wai paused to drink some coffee, then continued, "At this stage, Amilcar called Theo, Nab and myself to meet him. We met together and then all individually. Amilcar said he wanted trusted people around him to develop the coffee plantation, to support the workers and their families, to create educational programmes, and to do good for the planet. Basically, he introduced social enterprise built on the principles of profit, planet, and purpose. He said he would develop *Good Business,* by engaging both those he trusted, and those with *Passion* with a capital P.

That was the time we started the *Loving Little Lids Foundation*. We used ring-pulls from cans and linked them together. We used waste material to cover them and introduced zero deforestation leather and introduced other green principles. Ethics and transparency were what Amilcar wanted.

After a life of bullying and deceit, he wanted to cleanse *La Hacienda* and contribute to the world around him. He wanted to lift the lid off the bad and, in even the smallest of ways, he dedicated his life to start making a loving difference.

Hence the name, *Loving Little Lids Foundation*.

Amilcar always thinks in elevated ways. His spirit is pure. His DNA has nothing to do with his father. He has a heart of gold.

But he is sick. He has been sick ever since I have known him. He once told me he should have died at the age of 21, but he'd vowed to get the future of La Hacienda on track and to be responsible for doing good.

Any year after his 21st birthday, he considered it to be a bonus year.

He is now into was 34th bonus year, I think. He is around 55. He is the brains, Bika. The heart and the brains. Theo makes things happen, and he is a hell of a guy. But, in contrast, Amilcar has the heart of an Angel and the brain of an Einstein. Theo has the heart of a Robin Hood and his brain, well, in that he takes direction from our leader and inspiration, Amilcar."

I sat in silence for a while.

Then I said, "Did someone plant you next to me after I slept? How can you be telling me about the people in my life over the past thirty years? This just seems odd and I am not sure what to think."

"You do know what to think, Bika. I can see it in you. Your heart knows. Our paths were clearly meant to cross."

I pulled the Merino blush sweater which Bash had given me, over my head. I was flustered. I was wearing a long sleeved, low scooped T-shirt underneath. I had to cool off. I was at that age that hot flashes began. Maybe this was one. My cheeks felt as if they were on fire.

"Have some water," Wai said, screwing the top off the little water bottle which he had placed in the seat pocket in front of him.

"Thank you, Wai," I said, as I used the gold coloured elastic band, I had around my wrist, to whip my hair up into a pony-tail. It would help to reduce the heat around my neck. I pulled my shoulders down and arched my back, trying to remove the tension from between my shoulder blades.

"Bika, turn your back to me and allow me to touch your acupuncture points. It won't take me long. You should feel better if you allow me to apply some pressure on the relevant areas."

On reflection, perhaps it was weird, though I felt comfortable with Wai. What he'd just told me related to chapters of my past. And what I did not realise, though perhaps he did, my future too.

I offered him my back and said, "Sorry for turning my back on you."

"What do you mean?" Wai asked. "Why apologise for your back if I have asked for you to turn it to me."

"Oh sorry," I said, "force of habit. In the Middle East you should not present your back to someone. It is rude and inappropriate, much like showing the soles of your feet. If you enter an elevator and the only place for you to stand is in the middle, if the lift was full, you excuse your back."

"Understood. Now then, let's see."

Wai placed his firm warm hands and nimble fingers between my shoulders. It felt as if the tension between my shoulder blades was melting, as if winter was transitioning into spring. Wai moved up to my neck and shoulders. It was comfortable and there seemed nothing odd about this virtual stranger touching my skin and taking the tension out of my muscles. The necklace around my neck irritated me and I slipped it off over my ponytail. It got caught in my hair.

"I got you," Wai said. "Let me give you a hand and undo this knot you managed to create."

The leather lace was caught up and took some to unravel. Eventually Wai took the necklace over my head. I held up my hand, back to front over my shoulder, so Wai could put my necklace into my palm.

I sat there for a few seconds and then said, "Wai, let me hold that."

Wai didn't say a word for a while. Confused, I dropped my hand back down and turned round to face Wai. Having been overly hot, I was now verging on feeling cold. I slipped my sweater back on and released my ponytail to cover my neck with the warmth of my hair.

Wai held the little Mayan Jade Man in the palm of his hand. "It's you," Wai said. "He chose you."

Vaya con Dios

Amilcar was laid up in a bed placed in the middle of *Hacienda Sueño en el Cielo's* lobby. Both Wai and Nab had been and gone. They had spent mere moments with their friend. It was strange to see Wai and Amilcar together, but they were clearly connected.

How strange to have met Wai on the flight. And, at the same time, there was nothing more natural.

The monitoring equipment and wired devices had been disconnected from Amilcar. He looked frail and translucent like some fading impressionist painting about to dissolve. It was a surreal experience on the veranda. The coffee plantation stretched out into the distance like a sea of green, rolling into the blue of the Pacific Ocean beyond.

Amilcar gestured to me to come over to him. He looked at me and blinked once. As if I were summoned in the gentlest of ways. However, as I now realised, by a most powerful man.

Amilcar took my hand and looked at me.

Theo had been standing close by. He had been staring at nothing, his head lost in thought, by the looks of it.

Amilcar raised his eyes toward Theo, who turned to look at him. Theo understood from Amilcar's eyes what he was asking.

"Viv, have you got the Jade Man on you?"

"Yes, I always wear him."

Amilcar looked at me and turned his right hand with his palm upwards and rested it on his leg for support. He was asking me to give him the jade amulet. I retrieved the little jade man from his usual place between my breasts, and with the warmth still held inside the stone, I placed it in Amilcar's hand. He looked at the figure, put it to his lips and kissed it. Then he kissed the palm of my hand and placed the jade amulet in it, and whispered, "Vaya con Dios."

Theo looked away. Overcome. Then he turned back to Amilcar. Amilcar held his hands out. One towards Theo, the other towards me. Theo and I crossed over Amilcar's frame to link hands, forming a triangle, the most solid of any foundations. As we stood there, with tears in our eyes, looking down at our frail friend, I could smell the scent of the arriving rain.

The sun had disappeared behind the clouds and the heavy weather came rolling in off the Pacific. The rain started. First, a single drop, like a massive teardrop, followed by the initial ticking on the roof under which we stood. It felt as if the skies were softly crying. The rain picked up, and soon it was beating down. The howler monkeys pounded over the roof, across the plantation, seeking shelter. The lightning drew grizzly patterns on the darkened sky, followed seconds later by the loud sound of thunder.

Amilcar closed his eyes. Then he opened them once more. He looked at Theo and then at me.

With one last breath, as the loudest of thunders struck, Amilcar was gone.

I could see Theo crumble. He held on to his friend's hand, which was now limp though still warm. Theo held it to his face, putting the top of Amilcar's hand against his cheek. He started to sob. The rain kept pounding beyond the boundaries of this wall-less space. I walked up behind Theo. As he was bent over Amilcar's body, I stroked his blond hair. He could not see me cry. Amilcar and Theo were like brothers. It was not my place to show my grief. I had to be there for Theo. He was always there for us, consistently strong and decisive. I had not seen him distressed before. Annoyed, cross, furious, yes - but never sobbing like a boy who lost his family, all in one go.

I don't know how much time passed by, but as is the way of nature in Costa Rica, after the skies had opened and the downpour was complete, the sun reappeared. The clean and vibrant vegetation reflected the rays in the water droplets that covered each leaf and every creature after the rainfall.

After some time, Theo made the call. Within minutes the medical team, which had been with Amilcar over the past months, appeared. They respectfully covered Amilcar and took him away from the central lobby.

I put my arm around Theo, and he did the same to me. We walked over to where the balustrade was. The birds and the monkeys came back out to play as the sun reappeared. The leaves were still soaking wet. Over the bluff in the distance where the house of Curtis Coffee stood, a perfect double rainbow appeared.

"May God keep you in eternal peace, my dear brother," Theo said.

With that, he pulled me into him, like he always did. He held me under his arm and next to his heart.

We stood in silence for a while, then Theo looked at me. "Vivi, now Amilcar has left us, may God rest his soul, I need to talk to you. I have known this day was coming since the time we were living on the Mountain. Amilcar was born with the condition that slowly killed him. I thought it was a type of diabetes. I never found out exactly what it was, though it doesn't make any difference. He has gone. And for once, I realise that I cannot control the situation."

He looked away, then back at me, "He gave me a letter for you, Vivi." Theo passed me the envelope.

"Shall I read it? Or should I leave it for later?"

"I think it may be better to read it now, Viv. I knew he wanted to give it to you himself, though I don't know what it says."

"OK," I said, and I carefully opened the thick cream envelope with the Hacienda *Sueño en el Cielo* embossed on it.

We sat down next to each other on the long sofa in *La Hacienda's* lobby. I read the letter out loud.

'*Querida Vivika mia, thank you for being by my side. We locked hands all those years ago when we walked into the Ballroom at Le Montreux Palace. I held my hand out to you, and you took it. You asked no questions; you passed no judgement. You simply walked with me along the darkened aisle, our path lit by candles. It was Theo who told me you are like a sister to him. He made me laugh when he told me you are the only one who never showed an interest in him, other than as a close friend. He trusts you, and I respect his judgement. Theo may never tell you the truth, so I will do it for him. He trusts you, and I need to trust you too. I ask you to keep what I am about to tell you in confidence.'*

I looked at Theo. "Is it OK to go on?"

"Yes, Viv, maybe it is time for you to know the truth."

What did Theo mean?

I read on.

'All our fathers are art dealers and drug barons. When I say we, I mean the fathers of Theo, Bash, and myself. Theo won't mind telling you that his father was a dealer who was being investigated when he met El Comandante, as my father was known. My father was a relentless and ruthless trader in Pre-Colombian Art. He had entire networks and teams who robbed graves.

Theo's father and my father met through the network, connecting Europe with Central and Latin America. Later, they met Al Bashir, Bash's dad. He was the King of illegal trade in the Orient, moving artefacts, old mosaic floors, Ottoman relics and gold, and African diamonds. The three illicit traders, all-powerful men in their own corners of the world, used to meet up in various places where trade routes connect. One of the critical locations was Morocco. The desert was at the crossroads of Africa, the Middle East and Europe. After some years of trading together, Theo's father, Johan, met Bashir and my father. They realised they each had one son. They hatched a plan to create the next generation of traders. By doing so, when they retired or were fed up with travelling, their offspring would be able to keep their fortunes coming in.

The three decided to send Bash, Theo, and myself to the same school, on the Mountain in the middle of nowhere in Switzerland. They did not care whether it was a Hotel school or a girl's school, if we three were together in the one place. The instruction was for us to bond. No matter if we boys got on with each other or not. Our fathers demanded it.

I remember thinking that Theo was loud, and I was not at all keen on having to spend time with such a ladies' man. However, he proved himself to be caring. I could see his pure heart. He took care of me and looked out for me, and always has. I was never a threat to him regarding any of his women.

Most people thought maybe I had no interest in women. I am interested in genuine people, and you are a person who stays faithful to the truth. I know that is what Theo loves about you too.

As for Bash, what to say? He is bashful. He is not a bad guy, Vivi, but he lacks tenacity and backbone. He does not know his own self and sits on the fence. You cannot trust people who sit on the fence. While he is fun, he is confused and a little lost. Sometimes I see signs of hope. But over the past thirty years, Bash has pursued his wishes and lost people he loved by inadvertently putting them into harm's way. I hope you choose simply to be friends with Bash. Not more. Not less.

I won't keep talking about the past, especially since I have now left you for a new future. But to make sure that Hacienda Sueño en el Cielo remains loved and cared for, I am leaving the estate to you and Theo. The accumulated riches of art my father stashed here, I give to Theo. It cannot be traded to the network, but it can be sold for good, and it was there to support sound business under the Loving Little Lids Social Enterprise work.

When Theo gave you the little Mayan Man, it was by my instruction. I told Theo I wanted him to hang the magical amulet around the neck of a person he trusted and always would. Theo chose you. He has known for all this time that the shared ownership would be with someone he cares for.

The little Jade Man was stolen from a grave, just as Theo told you. Robbed artefacts bring curses. However, ones that have been cleansed with genuine love bring blessings. Your little man will always keep and protect you.

I will be cremated, and my ashes will be put in the large gold and jade vessel you see in the centre of the lobby. When you have my ashes, take the horses and ride down to the chapel. Use the bowl and leave it there, allowing the breeze to lift my remains with the eastern offshore winds to carry them out over the Pacific. Once I have flown away, make the best of the bounty La Hacienda offers.

I will see you in Paradise.

Know I will be looking down to see what magic you will create.

Vaya con Dios, amiga mia, and look out for Theo, like he does for you. Te quiero, un abrazo, Amilcar xxx'

Theo put his arms around me.

"He was my brother, Viv, and I have lost him. But he knew that you were my sister. It is up to us to follow through on his wishes, Viv."

"Lean on me sometimes, Theo. You don't have to take care of us all, all the time. I am here for you, as much as you are here for me."

"*Hermana mia*, my sister," Theo smiled, though tears were streaming down his cheeks.

"*Hermano mio*," I said, as I hugged him, as my tears soaked into his dark blue shirt.

Vibrate in Harmony

It had been a week since Amilcar passed.

His cremated ashes were returned home to *La Hacienda Sueño en el Cielo*.

Wai and Nab arrived on their horses. We took the jade, gold-edged bowl with us. Wai placed it sideways into one of the sustainable high fashion bags, designed under the Loving Little Lids brand. Theo held the urn with Amilcar's ashes, tucked under his left arm, where he kept it next to his heart. We, too, mounted our horses and rode through the coffee plantation, across the hills to the chapel. From there, the next high point that could be seen was Curtis Coffee's house. Curtis had passed some months ago, but I am pretty sure he was at the chapel in spirit.

In front of the little church, there was an al fresco altar with two torches the size of small columns. There was a gentle breeze blowing off the rolling green hills towards the Pacific. We dismounted our horses, and Wai took the bowl out of his rucksack and placed it on the altar. Theo set the urn on top of the bowl. We held hands and formed a circle around the rectangular altar, much as we had done with Amilcar when we formed our triangle over his death bed.

Theo spoke, "Our brother, Amilcar, you are our father. While we do not differ much in age, we stand worlds apart in terms of wisdom. You have entrusted us with your wishes. They are to do good. You told me to do the best we can to be clean. I recall your memorable message.

'Have the wisdom to know a tomato is a fruit, but understand it is not supposed to be put in a fruit salad.'

I think you were trying to convey that a person needs to make appropriate decisions that fit in with what is required. You then said that illegal trade is a sin but that if it can support people who cannot look after themselves, then the sin is lifted, just as in the case with the Mayan Jade Man. He was robbed from a grave but kissed and cleansed to be the catalyst for more incredible things. He symbolises wisdom, peace, harmony, and devotion to one's higher purpose. He helps whoever wears the amulet find their way and realise their dreams. Jade is worn to attract love and is given to another in the hope of obtaining love."

With that, Theo asked Wai for the little velvet sachet, which contained four jade marbles. He gave Wai, Nab and me one each and held one in his own palm. Then he pulled out a note that Amilcar had written and read it out to us.

'My three amigos and my one amiga, you have all the tools and means to make this world spin a little happier and shine a bit more brightly. You each hold a jade world in the palm of your hand. You are connected to each other. Let no planet spin alone. Be each other's sun for warmth and each other's moon for balance. Work together. Find your missions and do good. The antiquities can be traded or sold, even to those with ulterior motives, if it serves good in the end. I am trusting you to take forward what I envisaged, but could never achieve. I will be with you at every step. When you see me in the night sky or sense my touch on a sunny day, know that all the energy there ever was and ever will be, is there with you at that moment. Manifest miracles and they will be. The universe is infinite. Unblock yourself, be open, receive blessings. Call upon dormant forces of infinity and share the abundance. Vibrate in harmony. Amilcar xxxx'

Theo opened the urn and carefully emptied Amilcar's ashes into the jade and gold bowl. He placed it serenely on the small altar. It caught the setting sun, which reflected off its golden rim. The ashes lay there, thick, and still. We stood back, each of us with space between us, yet connected. We each held our little jade planet, symbolising our connection to Amilcar, each other, and greater things to come. Wai looked at me and gave me a gentle nod of closeness and friendship.

Theo placed the now empty urn underneath the altar. He came to stand beside me, all the while looking at the bowl. He looked anxious and tense. I held his hand. As I felt the warmth of Theo's palm in mine, a light breeze lifted and started to tease the ashes into the air. They rose and fell in the same place. As the breeze increased, the palm trees surrounding the chapel seemed to whisper.

A white-faced capuchin faced monkey climbed up a tree, and a sloth slowly descended. Two El Yiguirro birds flew overhead. The national bird represents the earth's fertility and is the symbol of rain. The Yiguirro sings at the beginning of the rainy season, which starts in April.

The green season was about to begin.

Just as the sun set, Amilcar's ashes lifted from the bowl and swirled into the air. Then, like the smoke from a pipe, they formed shapes and danced, dipping, and rising, settling into a pattern. They looked just like pixie dust as they floated in the direction of Curtis Coffee's house and beyond towards the vast expanse of the magical Pacific Ocean. Though Amilcar's ashes had been lifted and carried off on the current of the breeze, we all felt that Amilcar was still with us.

Full of Beans

The day after Amilcar's Ceremony, Theo and I were due to speak with Maddie, Bing, and Bash, or so I thought.

Theo and I were sitting at our worktable, which had been placed in the area where Amilcar's bed had stood on the day we had held hands, and Amilcar took his last breath. It felt like the right place to be working from.

The Hacienda's wall-less space was a magical spot.

The view over the estate and the Pacific Ocean in the distance was soothing. When the rains came, the thrill of continuing work while inhaling the scent of rain was energising. At the same time, it was incredibly grounding.

The table we sat at was made from an intricately carved door; it came from one of the old churches. The door had been placed on solid legs. On top of the door a heavy sheet of glass covered the carvings to create a smooth surface. But you could still see the exquisite flowers and birds sculpted into a single piece of tropical wood.

"Would you like a cup of our Amilcar's coffee before we call?" Theo asked me.

"I would love a Costa Rican cuppa," I replied while setting the laptop up to connect with Maddie, Bing, and Bash.

I was looking forward to seeing Maddie. It had been an abrupt departure. We had not spoken since our recent goodbye at Malaga airport, setting off on our separate ways. I was intrigued to hear Maddie's news and to share ours.

With our coffee in our hands, we connected continents. It was nice to see Maddie's face. She looked healthy, alert, and down to earth.

Happily pragmatic.

Bing looked like Bing, the same as I recently had seen him. I didn't know him, really, so I couldn't read the nuances. He appeared well enough. We exchanged hellos in a messy format where we all talked over each other.

"Where is Bash?" I asked.

"Ah, Bash," Maddie said. "Bash never turned up at the airport. I don't know why not. I wanted to call him, but I thought it would be best to check with Theo first."

As Maddie completed her sentence, Theo stepped in.

Although we were on a call together, Theo looked at me and ignored both Maddie and Bing when he said, "Vivi, Bash didn't show. He was asked to come to Morocco. I knew he was in potential danger, and we set a way for him to get out of Spain, but he didn't show up. Maddie was in touch with me from the airport to tell me that Bash wasn't there. I told Maddie and Bing to board their flight and make their way to *Al Trab Camp*. After that, I tried to contact Bash."

"Were you able to talk to Bash?" I asked Theo.

I forgot Maddie and Bing were listening in on the call. I just wanted to know what had happened to Bash.

"Viv, Bash didn't respond. So, I did some digging and ring-ing around. I found out that he was arrested by Interpol on his way to the airport. It was a long time coming. Bash got played by others and made some bad decisions. I had been worried about him for some time and sent him warning signals, which he ignored."

I looked at Theo, baffled. I couldn't really grasp the scenario playing out now in my mind, like a film, which Theo was presenting to me.

"Viv, I know you were not OK with me being so protective of you during our Reunion. You may have thought I was a spoilsport to keep interfering in Bash's pursuit of you. He is charming and fun, but, unfortunately, he has no backbone, Vivi. He is sloppy, undecided, and opportunistic. He allows excitement and possibility to lead him. The thrill of the kill for Bash gives him a sense of empowerment. His father always used Bash because of his fair looks but did not give him any credit as someone of value. You can see that person in Bash, and I think he is thrilled to be recognised as an individual. But he is too far gone, Viv. Too damaged. He will never be his own man. And he should never be yours.

He once loved a girl named Anna, but he used her too. She had to pay with her life. Bash said he could never forgive himself for that, but he never changed his behaviour, even after tragedy struck. Bash fell back into his old habits and his usual way of being. He doesn't know any better. I could have protected Bash for a very long time. He had his chances, warnings, and support, but he set himself up to be doomed. Now he has been caught.

While I am sorry to see it happen, it was inevitable. It almost seems as if Bash wanted to be taken out of this game, which he never chose, nor did he have any real idea how to play it. Bash will do his time and then go back to where he left off. He will be alright. Bashir Senior will want his blue-eyed Arab trade facilitator back.

But for you, Viv, you got off lightly. While it is hard to hear, you have been spared being trashed by Bash. I, for one, as well as Amilcar, God rest his soul, are determined to protect you from definite disaster. So, while I am sorry, I am grateful too."

I was quiet, trying to take in what Theo had just said to me. I knew in my heart that there had always been a question around Bash. He didn't show his inner self. Even in Switzerland and since the Reunion, there had been question marks all along the way. Obvious ones.

Still, this was quite some news to take in.

I sipped my coffee and heard Maddie start the conversation up again via Skype.

"Viv, I am sorry for you to hear this news now. But as Theo says, Bash will be fine. Try and move beyond what you can't help and take the good that Amilcar and Theo have seen in you. You are now able to do what you love, which is running *Good Business.* Look around you. You are in God's lap, Vivi. Count your blessings. Count them twice."

My mother's voice whispered her wisdom in my mind, quoting the Serenity Poem:

'Grant me the serenity to accept the things I cannot change, the courage to change the things I can, and the wisdom to know the difference.'

I took a deep breath in and smiled up at Theo, who hugged me.

"You go, girl!" Maddie encouraged me from the Skype screen.

Bing remained quiet. He knew he was not yet in the inner core circle where Maddie, Theo and I connected.

Feeling brighter, I asked Maddie and Bing about Morocco and how they were doing.

"The place is spectacular, Viv. Seven stars all the way but in a barefoot luxury type of tribal interpretation. Genuine and basic in its way, the place oozes class. Bing has done a great job."

Maddie smiled at Bing, but there was no sexual tension between them. That ship had sailed, it seemed.

"We need to re-group. For that, I need you here, Maddie. There are opportunities for us to consider in the desert. For now, Bing, hold the fort and stay where you are. Maddie, I would like to have you in Costa Rica over the next week to plot our course. Are you OK with that?"

Maddie beamed at Theo, "Are you kidding me?"

I could almost see their energies connect between the desert where Maddie was and the jungle where Theo stood next to me. It was electric.

The surge of positive vibrations and resonance sparked over onto me and created a pure sense of elation in the deepest parts of my soul.

I stood up and stretched.

Theo looked at me, as Maddie and Bing watched on. We were all smiles, no words.

I picked up my cup, half full, and I looked out over the fertile plantation and raised my mug to toast, "It's a jungle out there, but with our guiding star, we will move mountains."

With a loving acknowledgement to Amilcar up in heaven,

Theo raised his cup and said, "*Pura Vida.*"

"*Pura Vida*," we repeated, in unison, raising our coffee cups in Costa Rica and the teacups in the desert. We connected our continents. And with heaven above.

I took out my little jade man and looked at his engraved Mayan face full of love and wisdom.

I remember a quote that resonated:

'All the energy that ever was and ever will be is already here. Energy is never created or destroyed. What you want already exists. The kingdom of heaven is within you.'

With a sense of exhilaration, I kissed the little man and tucked him back where he belonged, next to my heart.

Full of beans, I was ready.

Next Chapter Ready!

Interview with the Author

Helen Van Wengen (Britt Holland) is a citizen of the world. That sense of wonder, sharing and positivity in the joy of cultural exchanges has been poured into a series of books which in part reflect different aspects of Helen's own remarkable life.

Born in Holland, Helen's childhood was in the Netherlands, with frequent visits to the UK, before she travelled to Switzerland to study hospitality at one of the world's top Hospitality Management Schools. There, Helen was introduced to friends and cultures as they lived, learned, and forged strong global friendships.

This experience shaped the young woman's life forever and set her on a journey that would see her work in the hotel industry worldwide, particularly in Europe and the Middle East and in Central America and Asia.

Now living between Jordan and Amsterdam, Helen is engaged in multiple projects, ranging from hospitality and tourism to social enterprise initiatives that drive profit for purpose, people, and planet. Helen believes in aspirational outcomes with a positive spirit. With her upbeat nature, Helen knows that miracles happen every day.

And on meeting Helen, it is the positivity that shines through. A positivity which has enabled her to boldly reflect on complex, wonderful and sometimes frankly hilarious parts of her life for a series of fun but savvy books which have echoes of *Eat Pray Love, Sex and the City and Four Weddings and a Funeral.*

Helen said: "The journey of writing these books has been so transformational because when I am writing, I feel as though I really am there while at the same time being able to reflect on situations and emotions I write about. And in some cases, remember as the words pour out.

"There have been times that I have cried and laughed, and those elements are all in the books".

"The books are not autobiographical, but there is so much of myself and my own experiences in the characters."

And the process of writing the books she said has fuelled and developed her soul and given her great joy.

Between The Sheets is a fascinating read, full of love, drama, sex and intrigue, supported by strong female characters that give the work a sense of empowered authenticity.

Helen said: "I love how my writing has connected my heart and mind to the past, made me more conscious of each day and allows my excitement of tomorrow to spill over on to the pages of my books. As a result of writing, I reconnected with amazing friends with whom, in some cases, I lost touch. One dear friend described my books as 'a magic carpet ride' that sparked a tear, a smile, and triggered thoughts she had forgotten all about. Touching other peoples' lives in positive ways matters to me. I will continue to live and write stories for others as well as myself. Living life is a privilege and one I embrace.

Also by Britt Holland

Between the Sheets
A story about life, lust and love

Vivika no longer feels like her former bubbly self. She was stuck in a rut. Overworked and exhausted. When a British naval ship docks in the port of Amsterdam, Vivika is compelled to attend a cocktail reception. Vivika isn't looking to be swept off her feet by the Captain of Her Majesty's Ship, *Carlington*. She can't help noticing that he seems able to manage her like no man has before. He intrigues her, but before long he sets sail.

When Vivika starts working for a luxury hotel chain with resorts in the Middle East, she soon realises she's joined a sinking ship. The owner, a prominent Arab businessman, is at loggerheads with the management company, and pins all his hopes and demands on Vivika.

With an ego larger than Burj Khalifa and a temperament more explosive than Vesuvius, His Excellency General Salim, does not take no for an answer. He stirs her in ways she didn't deem possible. With her loyalties divided between company and owner, Vivika plots her course. She negotiates the waves of passion, pain, and loss.

Will she survive the high Arabian seas with her true north intact?

Forever Connected

A story about good energy and forever friendships

Vivika, the hospitality professional from *Between the Sheets* who attended The Grand Reunion in *Mountains of Love*, travels to Costa Rica. Vivika finds herself co-owning a coffee plantation and meets handsome Humphrey. Against the vibrant backdrop of resplendent nature, Vivi embraces every Pura Vida day and her forever friendships. When Vivika attends the bi-annual Pussy Posse reunion in Portugal, old flame Bash, revs the powerful engine of his olive golden Aston Martin. Ready to go full throttle.

Printed in Great Britain
by Amazon